Flash and Bang

A Short Mystery Fiction Society Anthology

J. Alan Hartman, Editor

Untreed
Reads

Flash and Bang: A Short Mystery Fiction Society Anthology
J. Alan Hartman, Editor

Copyright 2015 by
Herschel Cozine: The Perfect Crime
Bobbi A. Chukran: The Conflagration at the Nameless Cotton Gin
Su Kopil: Murder on Elm Street
Pamela A. De Voe: Fireworks (From Judge Lu's Ming Dynasty Case Files)
Laurie Stevens: The Bag Lady
Tim Wohlforth: Sierra Noir
Suzanne Berube Rorhus: Thor's Breath
Sandra Murphy: Arthur
Julie Tollefson: Fractured Memories
O'Neil De Noux: Don't Let the Cop into the House
John M. Floyd: Rosie's Choice
JoAnne Lucas: Don't Be Cruel
Andrew MacRae: A Simple Job
Judy Penz Sheluk: Beautiful Killer
Albert Tucher: The Fruit of Thy Loins
Earl Staggs: The Raymond Chandler Con
Barb Goffman: The Wrong Girl
BV Lawson: Silent Measures
Walter Soethoudt: A Day Like No Other

Cover Design by Ginny Glass

ISBN-13: 978-1-61187-829-5

Also available in ebook format.

Published by Untreed Reads, LLC
506 Kansas Street, San Francisco, CA 94107
www.untreedreads.com

Printed in the United States of America.

Publisher's Note

CONTENTS

Introduction

In 1996, Margo Power, publisher of *Murderous Intent Mystery Magazine,* founded the Short Mystery Fiction Society.

In a few years, some members of the society started a magazine called *Mysterical-e.* Then they arranged to begin giving out yearly awards named the Derringers for short mystery fiction of up to twenty thousand words. Almost twenty years later, the society has grown to more than 1,600 members worldwide, *Mysterical-E* changed its name slightly and its publisher, but is still extant, and the society still gives out those Derringer awards annually. More information and links at the end of this introduction.

The Society celebrates short mystery fiction and welcomes anyone interested in the genre. Writers, editors, publishers and readers will find interesting discussions about writing, publishing, marketing, conventions, awards, the writing life and many other topics of interest.

This year the group decided that having an anthology made up of stories by members would be a great project. Jay Hartman from Untreed Reads volunteered to edit and publish the collection of stories that you now hold in your hands.

There are nineteen short stories by nineteen amazing authors all in one volume. Here's a peek inside:

1. "The Perfect Crime," a rhyming flash by Herschel Cozine, proves that crime writers can write the perfect crime story.

2. Was the fire at the old cotton mill arson? If so, who could have set it? Find out the surprising answer in "The Conflagration at the Nameless Cotton Gin" by Bobbi A. Chukran.

3. There'd been a "Murder on Elm Street" years ago, and the house had remained empty ever since. Until the power went out and two strangers moved in. A real mystery by Su Kopil.

4. In "Fireworks (From Judge Lu's Ming Dynasty Case Files)" by P.A. De Voe, what was supposed to be a celebration turns deadly.

5. If you like surprise endings, you'll love "The Bag Lady" by Laurie Stevens.

6. In "Sierra Noir" by Tim Wohlforth, the stakes are hot and high. A fire almost burns down a whole town, but a young woman loses her life to gunshots, not the fire.

7. Suzanne Berube Rorhus tells an unusual tale of two inventors that takes place in ancient times in "Thor's Breath."

8. Sandra Murphy provides laughs and surprises in her flash story, "Arthur." Don't miss it.

9. In "Fractured Memories" by Julie Tollefson, more than fireworks go off at a Fourth of July celebration.

10. "Don't Let the Cop into the House" by O'Neil De Noux is a powerful story about two police officers having an intense discussion, and what follows.

11. In "Rosie's Choice" by John Floyd, the suspense builds to unbearable heights while an old woman confronts two gangsters offering "protection."

12. A retro, atmospheric story about unrequited love is JoAnne Lucas's offering, "Don't Be Cruel."

13. Andrew MacRae's "A Simple Job" involves a detective, a beautiful female CEO and blackmail.

14. Another flash story, "Beautiful Killer," by Judy Penz Sheluk is a moving tale of love and loss.

15. There's Diana, the smart hooker whose heart of gold is a bit tarnished in "The Fruit of Thy Loins" by Albert Tucher.

16. Earl Staggs's story, "The Raymond Chandler Con," stars a smart sheriff and a brave best friend who disagree about how to catch a murderer.

17. A satisfying, flash revenge story is short and not so sweet—"The Wrong Girl" by Barb Goffman.

18. Then there's "Silent Measures" by BV Lawson, a heartwarming tale of a little deaf boy being lost, then found.

19. Walter Soethoudt's story, "A Day Like No Other," closes out the anthology with a look at a police lieutenant in Antwerp whose social intolerance leads to a *very* bad day.

SMFS blog: http://shortmystery.blogspot.com/
Mysterical-E: http://mystericale.com/

Jan Christensen
President, Short Mystery Fiction Society

The Perfect Crime
Herschel Cozine

"It's a murder most foul!" said the great Sherlock Holmes.

"I agree," Philip Marlowe replied.

"It wasn't the maid," said the taciturn Spade.

"She was gone when the old fellow died."

"And the gardener, too," said the pious Father Brown,

"He was praying in church at the time."

And the bleary-eyed Scudder remarked with a shudder,

"It's a gruesome, unsolvable crime."

"Yes, indeed," said Poirot. "I am baffled for sure."

Nero Wolfe uttered, "pfui" and grumped,

"Although we are blessed with the best of the best,

We are hopelessly, utterly stumped."

"We have done it!" exulted Sir A. Conan Doyle.

"We've outwitted our noble creations."

With a whoop and a shout, the unflappable Stout

Hugged Miss Christie with congratulations.

While Chesterton beamed in a satisfied smile,

And Chandler gave handshakes to Hammett,

The astute Mister Block, with his eyes wide with shock,

Muttered softly, "We did it, Goddamit!"

The Conflagration at the Nameless Cotton Gin

Bobbi A. Chukran

The anonymous letters were crude, almost as if a child had scrawled them. But that was no surprise given that most of the employees at the cotton gin were barely high school graduates. The notes were filed away and mostly forgotten by all but a few until after the fire. By that time, it was too late to use them for evidence.

On December 15, there was a flash fire at Nameless County Cotton—the largest the town had ever seen. The gin burned to the ground in a conflagration that sent three fire fighters to nearby hospitals suffering from smoke inhalation. One was airlifted to San Antonio and eventually died from third-degree burns after being in critical condition for over a week.

The day of the fire, Selma Riley reports that she was in her kitchen and heard a loud BANG and hurried outside to make sure the old Chevy hadn't fallen on her husband Roy. He'd been in the garage and was changing the oil and had the old car up on a makeshift jack. She ran to him and was relieved to find that he was fine.

They both ran back to the yard where they stood and watched a huge cloud of black smoke toward the east of Nameless. The Riley home was only a half-mile from town and the acrid smoke already filled the air and burned their eyes.

Selma flapped her hand in front of her nose. "Oh god, that smells awful. What in the world?"

"There's only one thing that smells like that; lord help us," Roy said. "Smells like the cotton gin's on fire." They watched as two fire engines from nearby counties raced by with sirens blaring. "It smells the same way the bedding plant did when it caught fire two years ago," he added.

Selma nodded. "Yes, I remember. That was horrible. I didn't get that out of my nose for weeks."

The cotton gin sat at the edge of town, beside a large network of railroad tracks, and processed all the cotton for over ninety farmers countywide.

Bucky Riley, ten years old, came running out to the road. "Oh boy! Would you look at all the fire trucks!" His eyes lit up as he watched them.

Before the night was over, it would take crews of forty firemen from surrounding counties over five hours to put out the fire.

Neighbors from up and down the street gathered to watch. Mrs. Theodora Staley said that it smelled like hellfire and brimstone—like the world was coming to an end.

"It's a good thing the place was closed for the holidays," Selma said. "Or more might have been hurt."

"Yeah, good thing," Roy mumbled, deep in thought.

Roy was quiet during dinner. Afterwards, he took his coffee to the living room, eased back in his recliner and picked up the *Nameless News*. He shook out the pages and read the headline—NAMELESS COTTON GIN TO CLOSE IN JANUARY. He threw it aside in disgust.

His wife turned off the light to the kitchen and joined him, taking a seat on the sofa. She nodded at the paper. "First the bedding plant, and now this. If I didn't know better, I'd think you were job-jinxed! Good thing we have some savings to tide us over."

Roy just grunted.

She reached over and took his hand. "Not that we don't like having you around the house. It's been nice lately, and you've had more time to play with Bucky. He loves having you here at home."

He didn't say anything and kept staring at the paper. Finally he sighed and the lines around his mouth made him look much older. "We've lost over three hundred jobs in this town alone over the last three years. I don't know how much more we can take. We had our suspicions after the layoffs last year that something was going on. But we thought that the downsizing would tide us over. We never dreamed they'd shut down the whole plant permanently. It doesn't matter now. No way will they rebuild it."

*

The next day, at the HAIR-WE-ARE Beauty Parlor, Selma overheard Jewel Moore, an older lady in town, talking to the hairdresser. "I wouldn't be surprised at all if it was arson, pure as day. Went up like a powder keg," Jewel said, then mentioned some cotton dust and sparks. Selma had no doubt it was true. After all, Jewel was dating Sheriff Lyndall Tinker, and probably had the inside scoop. And not only that, there was a rumor that somebody had been sending anonymous threats to the manager, but it was all "hush-hush."

Selma rushed home to tell her husband what she'd learned. "Roy!" she said, "Jewel Moore said that they think the fire was caused by some sparks and cotton dust that had built up during the last harvest. Some kind of spontaneous combustion. I wonder if they even bothered to clean the place after the fall harvest."

"You don't say," he replied. "And where did she hear that?"

"From the sheriff, of course," she said, looking thoughtful.

"That woman could talk the hind leg off a mule. What does she know about it?"

"They're dating. You don't think that Mr. Smith did something, do you? For the insurance?"

"What? No! Smith has just as much to lose as we do. The Smith family practically built that gin. He's dedicated his entire life to his workers, and supports the local cotton farmers. No way would he destroy it."

She smirked. "Well, he certainly didn't hesitate to lay off those people."

"He was forced to do that." He sounded angry. "You never know what people will do when they get pushed."

5

"Maybe. Sounds like he stirred up a lot of trouble either way. There was a rumor that somebody sent anonymous notes, threatening Mr. Smith."

Roy nodded. "Yeah, that part's true. Smith was trying to keep that quiet. He didn't want anybody to know about them, and didn't even report them to the police. Only a few of us foremen ever saw the notes, so we decided to keep it hushed up. I got the impression they were idle threats, just a few guys blowing off steam, mad about losing their jobs so close to the first of the year. Smith didn't seem too concerned about them."

"Well, what did they say? The anonymous notes."

He shrugged. "Nothing much. Stuff like 'you'll be sorry' or 'it'll be your own fault if anybody gets hurt'—just general threats from men scared for their jobs."

She shook her head. "It sure seems awfully suspicious, doesn't it?"

He nodded. "Yep, it does."

*

After breakfast the next morning, Sheriff Lyndall Tinker pulled up in front of the Riley house. Roy walked out to meet him and they shook hands.

"Somebody saw some of the older kids playing down there right before the fire. I don't suppose Bucky knows anything about this? Heard any of his friends talk about it?"

Selma glanced at her husband. "Bucky hasn't said anything about it," she said. "He doesn't usually hang around with that bunch."

Tinker smiled. "Oh, I know that. But you know how kids are, braggin' and all. Maybe he heard something. Bucky's a good kid."

"He hasn't said anything," Roy said.

The sheriff nodded. "Right. Just what I figured. Had to check it out, of course." He clapped his hat on his head and started to get back into his truck.

"Do they know what happened? How the fire started?" Roy asked.

"They're still investigating, but they're pretty sure it was arson. Probably some of those homeless people who break into vacant buildings over the holidays."

"You don't say."

The Sheriff nodded, then stared at Roy for a moment, got back in his truck and pulled out.

Bucky came out of the house and watched as the sheriff drove off. "What did he want?"

"He was asking about the fire. Wondering if you'd heard anything."

Bucky shook his head. "Nope. But I'm not sorry that place burned down."

"Bucky!" his mother said, "Why would you say something like that?"

Roy frowned. "Son, I don't have a job now, and lots of other men don't either. It's not going to be easy finding another one. I know you don't understand." He tousled his son's hair and turned to leave.

The boy nodded then frowned. "But you'll be home now, right?" he asked. "You'll have lots more time off now, right? To play ball and stuff? Just like after the bedding plant burned? You won't have to go back to work right away, will you?"

Roy slowly turned and stared at his son. "No, but I'm looking for a job and hope to find something very soon. Why do you ask?"

The boy shrugged and continued to play with his fire truck. He looked up at his father with his innocent blue eyes. "I dunno. It's just that Mom and I love it when you're here at home with us. I don't like it when you work all the time. And Mom's much happier now, too."

Roy glanced at his wife. "I don't like it either, son, but a man's gotta take care of his family. You'll understand when you get older."

Bucky thought about that for a moment. "But that fire was cool, huh? All those fire trucks!" He laughed. "And all that smoke! I like fires. I hope there're more."

"Bucky! Mind your tongue. What a horrible thing to say!"

"A lot of people were hurt in that fire, son. There's nothing cool or funny about that."

"Did they ever find out who sent those notes?" Bucky pushed his truck around for a moment then looked up at his father.

Roy got still. "What? What notes?"

His son shrugged. "Oh, I don't know. The ones that said 'If anybody gets hurt it'll be their own fault?'"

Murder on Elm Street
Su Kopil

The BANG reverberated throughout every house on Elm Street, startling the inhabitants and plunging them into darkness on an icy winter night. Cold wind sliced through the cracks and caulking of windows and doors in three of the four houses.

Mona Pearson in Number 1 searched for candles while keeping up a steady barrage of commands to her husband, Ralph, who took advantage of the power outage to chug back two more beers.

In Number 2, Emerson Creswell, successfully clawed his way through the maze of furniture, books, tools and discarded debris in every stage of rot that seemed to erupt from the floorboards and rain down from the ceiling. That he found a flashlight was a miracle in itself; that the batteries were dead, merely par for the course.

Elsa Dunn, in Number 3, had just laid down with a headache when she heard the boom. She ignored it as something not pertaining to her, until the frigid air found her beneath the heavy blanket. She flicked the bedside lamp in vain then stumbled on numb feet to the closet. She found a pack of matches in the worn smoking jacket hanging next to the fur coat she hadn't worn in a decade.

The power company couldn't get through on the icy roads. Hour after hour, the residents of Elm Street paced, shivered, and huddled under covers—waiting. By 9 p.m., the wind started flinging pellets of ice against their French doors and oversized windows, and they could no longer feel their limbs.

Emerson was the first to notice that not all the houses on Elm Street were dark. From his dining room window, past the tangle of trees and yard junk, he saw Number 4 glowing like a beacon in the forest. He pulled on a pair of rubber boots he'd dug out from under a pile of old pizza boxes, shrugged into the old leather jacket from his writing days, and shoved his head into a black knit cap, then climbed his way to the front door.

9

At the same time, Mona Pearson screamed at Ralph to "get back inside this house this instant." If she hadn't paused for breath, she never would have heard his grunt. "The old Vanderhall place got lights. I'm going over."

Elsa Dunn, in Number 3, couldn't believe it when she spotted a shadowy figure coming out of Emerson's house. It had to be Emerson but she hadn't seen him use his front door in eons. Then she noticed the Pearsons slipping and sliding down their driveway. What on earth was going on?

Mona glanced in Elsa's direction before following the two men down the street. "Wait," Elsa yelled, but, of course, they couldn't hear her inside the house. Already dressed in four layers and a coat, she waddled to the door and flung it open. The frigid wind kicked her in the face. Fighting back, she screamed "Wait!" again.

Emerson turned, then Mona. They waited a heartbeat, but the cold demanded they keep moving, and so they did, with Elsa playing catch-up all the way to the gates of Number 4. Here they paused and looked at one another. They hadn't visited Number 4, nor spoken to one another for that matter, in twenty-two years. In all that time, the house had remained empty, set back from the road on a little rise of land, while the trees crept up to cradle it within their limbs. But there was no denying now, as they stood at the open gates of the drive, the warm glow of light and life from within.

By the time they made their way up the steps to the entrance, the front door was open, spilling out warmth and light and silhouetting the figure of a young woman. "We've been waiting for you," she said.

The startled group glanced at each other with apprehension, and perhaps a touch of fear. Their last time together had been here in this house for the Vanderhalls' anniversary party—a celebration that had ended in murder.

Ralph Pearson was the first to move. He stepped out of the cold and into the foyer. "Got anything to drink?" he asked.

The young woman led the group to the double parlor. Unlike their own cold, electric hearths, a real fire blazed in the fireplace. The room was cozy and well lit by a generator humming somewhere in the distance. A man stood by the bar, nodding to them as they walked in.

"I'm Madigan, and this is my husband Tom." The woman couldn't have been much more than twenty, with dark hair worn loose to her shoulders. She had a clean, scrubbed look. No makeup, no jewels, just a simple blue sweater that matched her eyes, and soft denim pants.

"Excuse me." Emerson stepped away from the fire where everyone had automatically huddled hands outstretched. "What did you mean you've been waiting for us?"

"With the roads impassable and the power still out, there was really only one place to turn in your hour of need. Please…" She gestured to the same overstuffed sofa and chairs that had been there the night of the party twenty-two years ago. There was no sign of dust or mold, not even a musty smell. "Have a seat. Let me get you some refreshments."

"That's what I like to hear." Ralph Pearson dumped his considerable girth in the chair closest to the bar.

"Tom, I believe Mr. Pearson wouldn't object to a Jack on the rocks."

"That'll warm my insides." Ralph rubbed his hands together and smiled for the first time.

"And I just boiled a pot of tea." Madigan poured from a silver tray and carried the steaming cups to the sofa where Mona and Elsa sat, backs rigid, on opposite ends. Mona accepted the Earl Grey with a grateful smile.

Elsa shook her head. "I can't abide tea even in this weather."

Unruffled, Madigan handed the second cup to Emerson who nodded his thanks and stood with one elbow resting on the fireplace mantel. She returned to the tea tray and picked up a thermos. "I also made hot chocolate just in case." She poured the brown liquid into a mug and brought it to Elsa.

Elsa breathed in the chocolaty aroma. "Mmmm."

"I don't mean to be rude," Mona said. "When exactly did you move in? Neither Ralph nor I noticed any moving vans."

Madigan glanced at Tom. "Oh we just slipped in during the night."

Ralph laughed. "Got you there Mona, didn't she?"

"We've been here about a week." Madigan took a seat in a wing chair across from the sofa. "Our own things haven't arrived yet. Fortunately the house was already furnished. We planned to introduce ourselves, but as you can imagine, we had quite a bit of cleaning to do."

"Lucky for us you're here." Emerson set his cup on the mantel and picked up a heavy silver candlestick. The room grew quiet and all eyes turned to him. He awkwardly replaced the decoration. "Mind if I put another log on the fire?"

He asked Tom but it was Madigan who replied. "Please."

They all watched as he fed the flames, sending a shower of sparks up the chimney.

"It doesn't look like power will return anytime soon." Madigan lifted the teapot. "We may as well get comfortable. Refills anyone?"

Drinks were refreshed and politely sipped while the silence expanded to uncomfortable lengths.

"Still writing them books?" Ralph's loud voice startled everyone including the man to whom the question was directed.

Emerson shook his head. He had been discreetly moving the knickknacks on the mantel into a cluster on one end.

"How would he have time to? He's too busy these days collecting junk." Elsa had been watching Emerson out of the corner of her eye. She'd been trying to decide whether she thought the gray in his hair was distinguished or not.

"And how is your husband, Elsa?" asked Mona. "Still traveling, I take it."

Elsa turned to Mona with an icy smile. "My, what a lovely necklace. Is it yours?"

The air between the two women crackled with the tension of buried grudges.

"It is lovely." Madigan spoke from the wing chair. "I noticed it when you took your coat off. It must be awkward, all of you here again, under this roof. Oh, don't be surprised. The real estate agent told us of the house's history—about the murder. You were all here that night, weren't you?"

Again an uneasy glance passed between the guests.

Emerson cleared his throat. "We've failed to introduce ourselves. Yet it would appear that you already know us."

"I've done my research. Tom will tell you I've always liked a good mystery."

Tom remained in his position behind the bar, silent and still, except when refilling Ralph's drink.

"It's only natural," Madigan continued, "to be interested in what happened in the house you're to live in. You were best friends with Claudia Vanderhall, weren't you?" Madigan peered at Elsa over her cup of tea.

"We were close." Elsa shot a look at Emerson who turned away.

"To kill her husband on their anniversary." Madigan shook her head. "It's hard to understand. Did she talk about problems in the marriage with you?"

Elsa fussed with the hem of her sweater. "We didn't talk about such things."

Mona snorted into her teacup.

Elsa glared at her.

"An affair is a problem, ya ask me." Ralph set his empty glass down hard on the bar.

"Rafe Vanderhall was having an affair?" Madigan asked.

"Not Rafe." Mona looked at Emerson. "Claudia."

Once again Emerson found himself the center of unwanted attention. By this time, he had surrounded himself with a collection of objects, including an ottoman and various fire pokers. He tugged the collar of his shirt, his back stiff.

"Claudia asked for a divorce," he said. "Numerous times. 'Course, I shouldn't have told the police that. They found her prints on the candlestick. Not this one." He fingered the thick silver candlestick on the mantel. "But one like it. It was an anniversary gift from a guest, so, of course, her prints were on it. Rafe was hit from behind. Anyone wearing gloves could have done it. Her prints would still be there from when she opened the gift." The rigidness evaporated and he collapsed onto the ottoman with his head in his hands. "If only I hadn't begged her to get a divorce..."

The lights flashed then dimmed considerably. Madigan stood. "Tom you better check the generator, and I'm afraid the tea has gone cold. We won't be but a moment." She left with the teapot, trailed by her husband.

Elsa got up and knelt at Emerson's side. At this range, she could see the new wrinkles that went with the graying hair and decided they were distinguished. She wondered if he smoked a pipe now, and almost giggled at the thought.

"It was long ago." She patted his back. "That woman is awful for dredging it up again like this. You can't blame yourself."

"Really Elsa." Mona rolled her eyes to the vaulted ceiling. "Are you still carrying a torch after all this time?"

Elsa jerked away from Emerson like she'd been burned. Her cheeks flamed red.

"You didn't think it was a secret, did you?" said Mona. "Everyone knew you were in love with Emerson. We didn't need Claudia to tell us, although she did, you know. At least, she told me. We laughed about it behind your back."

"You evil witch." Elsa lunged, but Emerson grabbed her wrist. "Tell me," she said, "was that before or after you stole Claudia's necklace?"

Mona's hand flew to the diamond necklace dripping from her neck. "Why you—"

"Are you accushin' by wife?" Ralph sat up spilling his Jack Daniels.

"Yes."

"O-kay. Justcheckin'." He lapped up the whiskey dribbling down the side of his glass.

"You must have a nice stockpile of jewels by now," Elsa continued. "I remember every time we went shopping you'd come home with something you didn't pay for. Only we were too polite to call you on it. But the nerve, to steal the anniversary present from a dead man before he had a chance to give it to his wife."

The lights flickered then brightened, momentarily blinding the guests. When they had blinked the spots clear, Tom once again stood guard at the bar and Madigan was pouring tea into two fresh cups. The room had grown cold but no one got up to fan the embers.

Madigan handed hot tea to Mona and Emerson. To Elsa she brought another mug of steamy chocolate. "You look flush," Madigan said. "Are you coming down with something?"

"I'm fine," Elsa replied. "Just cold."

"Drink up then." Madigan returned to her seat, and Elsa did as she was told, not caring when she burned the roof of her mouth. The sweet chocolate tasted too good.

"There is one thing I wondered." Madigan spoke to the room at large. "Did any of you stay in touch with Claudia after she went to jail?"

"I should have. I wanted to." Emerson's face was pale and drawn. He looked ten years older since entering the house. "But I couldn't bear it. I needed a clean break so I could get on with my life."

"You call barricading yourself behind piles of junk getting on with your life?" asked Mona.

"Look who's talking." Elsa came to Emerson's defense. "The only difference is your junk glitters and costs more."

"At least I went to see Claudia." Mona caressed the diamonds at her throat. "It was after the hearing. I tried to be a friend to her but she told me to leave. Ask Ralph, he was there."

"Thaaat's true," Ralph said.

"And what about you, Elsa?" Madigan asked. "You said you were close. Why didn't you stay in touch with Claudia?"

"I did." Elsa blinked and slurped the last of her chocolate.

Madigan's eyebrows lifted. "You did? Then you know what happened to her?"

"What happened to Claudia?" Emerson's teacup was on the floor in front of him, along with two books he'd found somewhere, and a pillow.

"She's still in jail, of course." Elsa waved her hand.

"No, she's not." Madigan's voice was clear and sharp. "Claudia is dead. She was convicted of a murder she didn't commit and thrown in jail. Eight months later she died."

"Dead?" Emerson rose to his feet stepping on the teacup and shattering it. "How?"

Madigan also rose. "None of you have any idea who I am, do you?" She stared at each of the guests. "I am Madigan Vanderhall, Claudia's biological daughter. My mother died giving birth to me in jail."

Mona gasped. "What are you talking about? Is this some kind of trick?"

Madigan turned on her. "I believe that diamond necklace you're wearing belonged to my mother, and rightfully belongs to me."

16

"Ralph." Mona stood. "Are you going to let this woman talk to me that way?" She glared at her husband who snored softly in his chair.

Madigan, the charming hostess, had transformed in front of them—a rebellious, vindictive teenager bent on getting her way.

"My mother didn't kill my father." She paced the room, her hands punctuating each of her words. "I knew it, but I had to be sure, which is why I brought you all here. The bad weather was timely, wasn't it? A gift from mother, perhaps. And did I mention Tom is an electrician? Creating a power outage wasn't a problem for him. We knew you'd be forced to leave your cold houses eventually."

"I don't understand." Elsa struggled to her feet. "What do you want from us?"

Madigan stopped pacing. "I've long suspected who the real killer was. And my theory was proven by what I heard when I left the room just now. That necklace was a gift from my father. Only as you said, Elsa, he never had a chance to give it to her. It was in his pocket when he was killed, wasn't it? You, Mona, were the first person to discover my father's body, not my mother like the police records stated. Only you couldn't resist your own greed. If you stole the necklace, who would know? A dead man could tell no tales. However, you forgot one other person. The killer knew about the necklace too. She said as much in this very room, isn't that right, Elsa?"

All eyes turned to Elsa who was trying to speak, but could only gasp like a fish without water. Her hands clawed at her throat, her skin turning an ugly shade of blue.

"You were jealous of my mother and Emerson so you told Rafe about their affair, only it backfired, didn't it?"

Elsa collapsed to the floor. No one moved to help her.

"As I said." Madigan smiled. "I did my research. Elsa wouldn't drink the tea. It was easy enough to poison her hot chocolate." Madigan turned to Mona. "Your husband won't remember any of this, at least nothing of importance. And if *you* tell anyone, you'll find yourself facing first-degree robbery with a max sentence of life in prison."

Mona eased away from the fallen Elsa and moved closer to her loathsome, pathetic, drunken husband.

"And you." Madigan turned to her mother's lover. "Daddy dearest. Are you wondering if I'm from the fruit of your loins—your only child? Well, there's only one way to find out, a DNA test, which I'll never agree to. Still, you won't speak about what happened here tonight, on the fifty-fifty chance that I am your flesh and blood, will you?"

Emerson stood, surrounded by his walls of clutter, staring at the woman who could be his child, and then at the dead woman on the floor, and slowly shook his head.

The fire gave one last desperate hiss then faded to black.

Fireworks (From Judge Lu's Ming Dynasty Case Files)

P.A. De Voe

The red silk lantern's flame glowed in the early morning darkness as Magistrate Lu and his younger brother, Fu-hao, sat in amiable silence, enjoying their breakfast. The sweet, fresh air spoke of spring. Fu-hao picked up his bowl of rice gruel and took a sip. Without warning, a sharp explosion broke the peace. Startled, he nearly spilled the thin white liquid onto his navy blue robe. Brilliant sparks of light danced over the top of the yamen's courtyard's wall, filling the lower sky.

"Even when we know it's coming, it's a surprise," Lu said.

"Rockets are a serious business. People shouldn't be able to shoot them off," Fu-hao groused.

Before he could continue, they were overwhelmed with short bursts surrounded by the rat-a-tat-tat of popping and crackling noises. Intense flashes of light rapidly appeared and disappeared.

"That's what I mean. Really, the Emperor should forbid rockets."

"Celebrating the monk Li Tian and his invention of today's fireworks shouldn't be discouraged," Lu said. "It's important to our people. The noise chases away ghosts and all that is evil, and the smoke cleanses everything. Together they bring peace, health and happiness."

After another round of sound and light pulsated through the courtyard, Lu sat back and added, "I only hope we don't have any fires with all this celebrating. I told the city security units to be prepared..."

"Sir," a voice called out. Ma, Lu's guard, strode into the lantern's light. "The city headman is here."

"Send him in," Lu said.

An elderly man with a sparse beard shuffled into the room. The city headman was an elder in the community and oversaw much of the city's day-to-day activities. When problems arose, he solved them; or, if the problems were serious, he brought them to the magistrate.

Once the elder had successfully ambled up to Lu's table, he stopped, bowed, and said, "Your Honor, I have unfortunate news to relate." He paused. "The Liu brothers from Hunan Province have a shop on Xiao Di Road. An apparently successful shop."

"And, so, what's the problem?" Lu asked.

"There has been an accident. Most inauspicious. Especially today. Most inauspicious."

"Yes?"

"I have to report that this morning, when the Liu brothers were setting off fireworks, something went amiss, a rocket exploded, instantly killing the elder brother, Liu Shih-kuei." He finished with his words tumbling over each other as though even speaking them would heighten the evil of such a death.

*

Lu, and his entourage of Fu-hao as court secretary, and Ma Jie and Zhang Chieng, his personal guards, rode through the tumultuous streets to the Liu brothers' shop. The ferocity of firecrackers erupted all along their route. Smoke enveloped them, cutting off their air, making it hard to breathe and stinging their eyes. Children ran laughing from one cascading pandemonium to the next. Lu worked to sooth his fearful horse as it tried to escape the gauntlet of noise.

In spite of the bedlam, Lu's mind never veered far from the scene he feared would greet them—a body mutilated by a rocket. His stomach churned and bile rose in his throat. He tightened the horse's reins.

Soon they arrived at a weathered building with a multilayered tree of spent firecrackers leaning against its wall. A clerk appeared, solemnly welcomed them, and led them into a dim back room. As Lu's eyes adjusted, he saw a beefy, sun-burned fellow lounging under the only window. Another—a thin, young man, sitting immobilized behind a tall desk—rested his hand on an abacus near a closed ledger. As Lu entered, the man looked up with eyes as hollow as empty wine cups. He appeared to be in shock. Nevertheless, when Lu approached—wearing his official robes with its large, square, magistrate's badge of office emblazoned on it—the young man jumped up, rounded the desk, and bowed deeply.

"Your Honor," he said and stopped, as if at a loss for words. His eyes flitted toward the window and back to the judge.

Lu glanced out the window. The early morning sun cast a long shadow over a narrow courtyard. Two lone potted trees marked the far corners.

A clerk brought a chair for the magistrate. Fu-hao took over the desk, preparing to record the interview for the court's report. Ma and Zhang stood at the door.

Shih-hua first introduced the other visitor as Ying Ren, a member of the Hunan Province's Merchant Association, there to help organize the burial details. Then, Shih-hua recounted the morning's drama, his voice low and deferential.

"My brother and I arrived at the shop well before daylight. We wanted to set off the fireworks exactly at sunrise. He thought that would be the most propitious time for our business. He'd recently returned from our hometown and brought back the most amazing fireworks display, and even a rocket. I wasn't sure about the rocket's safety. But it's what he wanted. He'd bought it at a very good price." Shih-hua linked his hands in front of him, sighing. "He was quite delighted with it."

"You didn't think it was too dangerous for him to ignite the rocket himself?"

Shih-hua shrugged and repeated. "It's what he wanted. He's my older brother; he decides—decided—what we should do."

Lu nodded. Of course, that was what tradition dictated, although he knew plenty of families where it was the more capable, not the oldest, who made decisions. Nevertheless, he said, "I see. Go on."

Shih-hua took a deep breath. "The clerks and I went into the street to light the firecrackers."

"Both clerks went with you? Your brother was alone?"

"The fireworks display was massive. I needed both men to help. Shih-kuei didn't need anyone; he only had one rocket.

"As I set off the fireworks I heard an explosion from inside. We rushed back, hoping to catch a glimpse of the rocket's fire and light." He frowned. "Too late, of course. I didn't realize how quickly it was over."

"And that's when you found him?"

"My brother lay on the ground, blood everywhere. The rocket was defective and exploded." Shih-hua covered his face with his hands. Recovering, he added, "I immediately sent one of the clerks to the city headman to report the accident."

Lu glanced at the large man near the window. "And you alerted the Hunan Merchant Association?"

Shih-hua nodded. "They handle the burial plans."

Nothing new there. Most merchants belonged to their home area associations, which provided both practical benefits and a ready pool of friendship when a man found himself living far from home.

"Why did your brother go home?" Lu asked.

"He went to celebrate his second son's one-year birthday. I stayed here because we couldn't afford to close the shop."

"How long was he gone?"

"Three months."

"Isn't that a long time?"

"I was here, he didn't have to hurry. I could take care of the shop, and he wanted to spend time with his wife and children."

"Are you married?" Lu asked.

Shih-hua clasped his hands together and said, "I have a wife but no children as yet. She lives with my parents and cares for them."

"Where does your older brother's family live?"

"With my parents." Shih-hua looked him straight in the eyes. "We are a strong family. We live together and work together. As is proper," he finished.

He examined the young man before him. The large family—consisting of married brothers, their wives, and children living together with the elderly parents in one household—was the ideal. However, real life pressures of equitable sharing of responsibilities and resources, not to mention the clash of personalities, often made such an arrangement difficult to impossible. He wondered how close the Liu family actually fit the ideal.

"You can be commended on your family's virtue," Lu said.

"Thank you, Your Honor," Shih-hua said, head down, hands clasped in a white knuckled grip.

*

Out under the courtyard's veranda, a covered body lay on a slab of wood. Blood splatters told Lu where he died. A table and chairs for the judge and his secretary had been set up on the surrounding wooden porch, outside the bloodied area. After Fu-hao had arranged his writing implements and taken a seat, Lu approached the body and turned back the cloth. As he feared, the body was badly burned with multiple injuries.

Ma removed the corpse's tattered clothing. Taking a knife, Lu paused, took a deep breath, and proceeded. He dug into several of the wounds and extracted iron pellets and broken pieces of porcelain. Stretching, he studied the courtyard's walls and porch columns. He walked to the area closest to where the rocket was detonated. A pattern of small holes spread across the wall. Again, using his knife he dug into the wood and removed more iron balls and bits of porcelain.

Standing with hands behind his back, he looked over the enclosed bare patch of dirt. He reconstructed the early morning scene: Shih-kuei alone when he set off the rocket; the others out front, preparing the firecracker display.

Running his fingers over the holes in the wall and posts, he noted their pattern.

"This was no celebratory rocket," he said to Fu-hao. "It was a bomb, disguised as a rocket and designed to mutilate and kill. It came from a military arsenal."

Fu-hao paused, his brush resting on the inkstone. "How could a merchant get such a thing?"

Lu slowly made his way around the veranda looking for areas where the bomb's contents had struck. He stopped at the table, silent, lost in thought.

"We'll need to interrogate everyone," Lu said. "Ma, bring the clerk who attended Liu Shih-kuei on his trip to Hunan."

Lu settled in the chair on the veranda near Fu-hao, facing out into the courtyard's neglected space.

A shaken, middle-aged man entered and stood on the bare ground below Lu. He bowed.

"I am Clerk Hao, and have been serving the Liu family for more than twenty years. I started under their father, Master Liu, and later worked for his sons when Master Liu retired."

"Have you always worked here in the city of Pu-an, in Jiangxi Province, or did you work in a city in Hunan Province?"

"When I clerked under Master Liu he had a shop in Pu-an but not here," his lips turned down. "Master Liu had a large building on the main road. His sons had to move to this small shop on Xiao Di Road last year."

"Was there a problem with the business?" Lu asked.

The clerk nodded. "The brothers had to move or close their business entirely."

"What happened? Our town is prosperous and the original shop was in a good area. What caused their business to have such bad luck?"

The clerk shuffled from one foot to another, then said, "The oldest son, Shih-kuei ran the business. Unfortunately, he had many debts and spent most of their profits." He again shifted his weight and glanced away.

"How?" Lu asked.

"Shih-kuei had expensive habits. He caroused and was well known at the brothels. He was rarely here. Shih-hua takes care of the everyday business, but it's like a minnow swimming upstream."

Lu continued, "Do you know where Shih-kuei bought the rocket?"

"No. I didn't know he had one. He bought a large firecracker display, but I don't know about the rocket. I thought they made him nervous. But...maybe he wanted extra good luck for their business this year."

Bad choice, Lu thought.

After the clerk left, Lu ordered Ma to bring in the second clerk.

A boy just reaching his manhood stepped into the courtyard. His round face had little color and his eyes darted around and finally halted at Lu's chest, fixating on the brilliantly colored magistrate's badge. He bowed low and deep.

"I am Clerk Tsai from Jiangxi Province. I began apprenticing for the Liu family five months ago. This morning we started setting up to celebrate Li Tian well before daybreak."

"When did you come in?"

"I sleep at the shop, so I was here when the Liu brothers arrived."

"What do you know about the fireworks?"

"When Master Shih-kuei returned from Hunan they stored the firecracker display in a room behind the courtyard. I never saw the rocket until today."

"Who brought the rocket in and set it up?"

The young man closed his eyes as if seeing the morning's events. "Master Ying brought in a large box yesterday. Master Shih-hua and he went into the back room. I heard them opening the box. I didn't hear what they said because their voices were too soft."

"Was Shih-kuei with them?"

"Master Shih-kuei was out." He cast a quick glance at the door to the shop. "He was at a wine shop yesterday and didn't return until this morning." He stopped and bit his lip as if reviewing a play. "I didn't think he would ignite the rocket, because when he found out about it this morning, he wasn't happy."

"Wasn't happy?" asked Lu.

Tsai nodded. "Master Shih-hua said they had to set it off, to improve business. They needed all the good luck they could get. There was an argument over who would ignite it. Shih-hua insisted Shih-kuei had to ignite the rocket since he was the older brother; it wouldn't be as auspicious if a younger brother did it. Eventually, Shih-kuei agreed.

"And now he's dead," the young clerk finished in a barely audible tone. "Bad luck."

When the boy left, Judge Lu ordered Master Ying enter for questioning.

The burly man strode into the courtyard and bowed quickly to the judge. Hard eyes looked out of a face with an intersecting set of scars on his left cheek.

"I am Ying Ren of the Hunan Province's Merchant Association. I came to the city looking for a job. I'm from Hunan but had traveled some before coming here."

"Where did you live before coming to Pu-an?" Lu asked.

Ying licked his lips. "I lived in Shaanxi Province for a few years. Another association member, who had also lived in Shaanxi, offered me work as the association's security guard.

"I'm acquainted with the Liu brothers through our group, that's all."

"Why are you here, at the shop?" Lu asked.

"Liu Shih-hua sent a message to the hall and I came to fulfill the Association's responsibilities in assisting in the funeral rites. It's the first time I've been to their shop."

Lu leaned forward and demanded, "What about yesterday?"

Ying's face twitched. He said, "I was here yesterday. I forgot. It wasn't important. I delivered a box to the shop."

"What was in the box?"

"I don't know. I simply delivered it."

"Don't lie to the court," Lu thundered. "You were here and opened the box. If you don't tell me now, I have ways to learn the truth."

Ying stared at the judge, then spat on the ground. Ma lurched forward, his staff readied to slam into Ying. Lu instantly raised a hand to stop his guard. Ma halted mid-step.

"Speak!" Lu ordered.

"I brought a box to Liu Shih-hua yesterday," he began sullenly. "Someone, I don't know who, left it at the Association's hall with a note to deliver it to the Liu shop. I didn't know what was in it until Shih-hua opened the box. It was a rocket. That wasn't a surprise. A lot of people are setting off rockets today. I didn't think anything of it."

As if to corroborate his story, the courtyard throbbed with another round of sharp bursts. Lu ignored them.

"Tell the court about your military experience."

At this, Ying started, eyes wide. "How did… Alright. Yes, I had a small problem with the law and was sentenced to military duty for six years, stationed on the Shaanxi border."

"And that's where you had access to rockets and bombs."

Ying began to spit again, glanced at Ma with his staff, and swallowed. "I did my time and came back to Hunan, but people don't forget the past. I eventually came to Pu-an and settled here. Except for the fellow I told you about, no one knew about my military experience."

"Except Shih-hua," Lu said.

"Except Shih-hua. Shih-hua married my sister. She carelessly told him about me one day. No one wants an ex-convict in the family, so Shih-hua never told anyone. But he remembered," Ying added bitterly.

"You sold the bomb to Shih-hua," Lu stated.

"It's my bad fate."

Lu ordered Ma to bind Ying's hands and Zhang to arrest Liu Shih-hua for his older brother's murder.

*

Back in the yamen's office, Lu sat drinking tea with Fu-hao, Ma, and Zhang.

"How did you know Ying had been in the military?" Fu-hao asked.

"He said he was from Hunan but had lived in Shaanxi Province. He's not a merchant. Therefore, what would take him to such a remote area? The Emperor has a large army stationed along the border to protect the country from the Mongols. Many of those soldiers are criminals serving out their sentences. It was a reasonable deduction." Lu took a sip of his tea.

"Ah," Ma said, "then the connection with the bomb became obvious." He smacked his lips.

Fu-hao's face tightened and he shot an irritated glance at Ma. Lu hid a grin. He knew his brother felt Ma and Zhang took too many liberties.

"But why did Shih-hua do it? Why kill his older brother?" Zhang asked.

"That's the saddest part of all. With their father retired and sick, the older brother had all the power and authority of running the family and their business. He was destroying the family."

"Making killing Shih-kuei seem the only solution," Zhang said.

"But an older brother," Fu-hao lamented. "That's a crime against nature."

Lu glanced at his younger brother, his confidant and court secretary, and counted his blessings.

The Bag Lady
Laurie Stevens

I needed the Orange County Line, but for the life of me, I could not work the stupid kiosk that dispensed the tickets. Taking a deep breath, I stepped away from the ticket vending machine. If I didn't, I might smack it with my hand. Although Union Station in downtown Los Angeles was filled with people, I felt utterly alone and helpless.

I had to board the 5:00 pm for San Clemente and it was already 4:45.

"Just pick a number and the routes will come up," I heard a voice behind me say.

I turned around to see an older woman standing a few feet away from me. From the ragged looks of her, I could tell she was a street person, a bag lady.

"If you click on a number," she told me, "it will tell you the route. Then you can pick the one you want."

I mumbled thanks and turned back to the machine.

The woman was right. I pressed a number, picked my route, and paid. Lo and behold, I watched the ticket drop into my hand.

The woman smiled. Her teeth had brown and yellow stains on them. "It's Track Four. Just follow me. I'm heading there myself."

I didn't really believe her, but followed her anyhow. That's how desperate I am these days. Can you imagine a successful sales executive for a wholesale company so down on herself she would follow the advice of a possible mental case? If I ended up at a garbage bin with a date to dumpster-dive, I probably deserved it.

But we arrived at Track Four and, according to the others waiting on the platform, this was the right place for the train to San Clemente.

I let go a big sigh and turned to observe my benefactress. I couldn't really decipher her age. Her hair was gray and messy. Her skin was thick-looking and carved with wrinkles. Her clothes were shabby—a housecoat covered by a damaged cardigan, covered again by two scarves. Only her eyes seemed youthful. She had bright blue eyes that shined with surprising clarity. Those bright eyes made me wonder how and why she was homeless.

The woman held on tight to one of those rolling baskets that stand vertically. In the tall basket were stacked various bags, some paper, some plastic, but mostly woven, reusable bags. She had a pile of them.

"Listen," I began gently. "Can I give you a couple of dollars for helping me out?"

A whistle drowned out my voice. The Metrolink train arrived with the pomp and bustle that should accompany a train's arrival. The people surrounding me bristled with anticipation and soon crowded in-between the bag lady and me.

I looked for her briefly, feeling a bit ashamed for not handing her a few bills when I had the chance.

But then I was on the train, looking for a seat near the window. Happily, I found a quartet of seats completely unoccupied. That suited me fine. I had my iPod and ear buds and planned to calm my quaking disposition by listening to music.

I welcomed this getaway. I was in the midst of an ugly divorce and needed a weekend to myself. I brought out my music, leaned back, and closed my eyes.

My mind wandered back to the bag lady. The streets of Los Angeles were no place for a vulnerable woman. No doubt she'd come from Skid Row on Fifth Street. Union Station was close by and easy pickings for panhandlers. But Fifth Street, along with the rest of downtown, was becoming gentrified. Decrepit "per hour" hotels were getting made over into luxury condominiums. Trendy cafes were opening on every corner in the hopes of attracting young professionals and celebrities. The unkempt and forgotten souls were being squeezed out.

I felt the train rumble around me and let myself relax. I might have dozed off, I'm not sure, but when I opened my eyes, I jumped in my seat.

There, in the seat across from me, sat the bag lady.

She was calmly appraising me with her bright eyes. Her rolling cart stood sentinel at her side.

My eyes roamed the car. What was she doing here? When did she board the train? I also noticed that our car was nearly deserted (perhaps because of her).

"I didn't realize you were boarding the train," I said.

"Sometimes they ask for your ticket. Sometimes they don't," she explained.

I didn't quite follow her reply, but I took it to mean she didn't have a ticket. Not having a ticket would hurl me into a frightful panic, but she didn't seem bothered in the least.

"Where are you going?" I asked her.

She shrugged and grinned. "Nowhere special."

I might have guessed that. Imagine having no other purpose than to live in the moment. For a second, I envied her.

"So..." I reached into my purse. "I want to thank you for helping me."

I pulled out a five-dollar bill from my wallet and handed it to her.

The bill quickly disappeared within her cardigan and she said, "Oh, bless you. Bless you."

Feeling as if I'd done a good deed, I decided to take it one step further and strike up a conversation.

"I don't know if you are interested," I told her, "but there is the Downtown Women's Shelter right on Los Angeles Street. I know about it because I've donated to it."

The lady regarded me blankly.

"The people there can help you."

She sighed and looked out the window. "They won't take me because of Larry."

"Who's Larry?" I asked, surveying her. "You have a pet? A dog?"

"Larry is my husband."

"Oh." I looked about the coach. "Where is he?"

"He's around. He's never very far away."

"Well," I began. "There are places that take couples, I'm sure. Would you like me to help you find one?" I got out my cell phone to access the Internet.

The lady shook her head adamantly. "No one will take me because of Larry."

I paused, looking at her, and then put my phone away.

Something must be wrong with Larry, I thought. Some of these homeless folks needed medication. Perhaps Larry was the kind of man who held animated conversations with himself, conversations that scared other people. I looked around the coach once again.

I didn't want to sit near Larry.

"So your husband acts in a way that prevents you from seeking help?"

Why was I probing this woman? I guess because I had a private grudge against my own husband, who I had caught cheating on me with my chiropractor—a woman whose back I'd like to break.

"Why don't you just let him alone and take care of yourself?" I asked, still thinking about my chiropractor.

The woman scratched her matted hair. "I can't leave Larry."

The train made a couple of stops and the passing scenery went from city to industrial. I kind of wished the homeless woman would get off the train, but she continued to sit across from me.

"You want to know how we met?" the woman asked me after we left the Norwalk station.

"Sure," I said, looking out the window. If she got weird, I would have to move to the next railcar.

"You know Beverly Park?"

"Beverly Park Estates?" Thinking of mansions, I turned to look at her.

The woman rolled her blue eyes. "No, Kiddieland."

My mouth fell open. I hadn't thought of *that* Beverly Park for years. Beverly Park, affectionately known as "Kiddieland" and its next-door neighbor Ponyland, once stood on the site of the fancy Beverly Center Mall. It had closed many years ago—sometime in the mid-nineteen-seventies.

"We met on the scary ride," the bag lady told me. "He hopped into the seat next to me. I didn't mind. He was kind of handsome. Oh, the ride wasn't scary, just a few fake monsters that leaned out at you, but I found myself holding Larry's hand just the same. We were only teenagers then, but I knew he was going to be the one I stayed with forever."

I have to admit I was a little entranced by the woman's story. For a street person, the woman was clear and lucid, plus she was providing me a piece of Los Angeles history.

She went on. "We continued to meet at the Park. There was a carousel and a hotdog stand, and a little train. Most of the rides really were for young kids, but we liked going just the same. Life wasn't easy at my house, so I got away a lot. Larry, he came from a better family, but he liked me, so he'd meet me there anytime I wanted."

"Wow," I said. "You and he have been together a long time."

She nodded. "Oh, yes."

"Then what happened? Can I ask why…"

I trailed off. I didn't want to be rude. It wasn't any of my business to inquire as to why two young people would start off fresh, with their whole lives in front of them, and then end up on the streets with all their worldly possessions tucked into a single rolling cart.

"Larry and I had a nice life for a while," she told me, apparently willing to share her history. "He worked for the city. He was a water utility maintenance man. He serviced water mains and fire hydrants, things like that."

"That sounds like a decent job."

"It was. It had good benefits, too."

Then what *happened*? I was dying to ask her. As if reading my mind, she answered for me.

"The problems began when Larry began to drink. We both had a taste for it. Me, I was used to it because my daddy used to drink, and my granddaddy before that. I guess booze is just in our blood. But Larry, he was more refined. The liquor got to him easier. He became mean."

I shuddered. I knew where this was going. He'd probably started to beat her or something.

"Were you abused?" I asked quietly.

She nodded. "One night, it got real bad. He got me with a knife."

She pushed up the sleeve of the cardigan. On her bare arm, I made out the line of a nasty, two-inch-long scar.

"I can't blame Larry," the woman said. "I've done bad things, too."

She pushed her sleeve back down, but the memory of that scar stayed in my brain.

"Why did you stay with him?" I asked, thinking about my cheating spouse and the divorce.

"He's all I have in the world, girly!"

The outburst surprised me. The woman looked a little nutty, so I backed off.

The train stopped at Buena Park, home to a somewhat grander amusement park, Disneyland, and then rumbled south once more.

I looked at my unwanted companion and considered moving to another seat. I so wanted to relax, but I couldn't. Instead, I kept a lookout for abusive Larry. I didn't discount the possibility of two thieves, either. Two scam artists who might like preying on the naiveté of a Good Samaritan. Maybe that's why this woman was sticking close to me. To set me up for her husband to come in for the kill. Again, I thought that maybe I should move to another car—one with more people in it, but I didn't.

I wish I had.

An announcement came on the train, which advised the passengers to ready their tickets for the conductor. I gave the woman a look, knowing she didn't have a ticket.

She grinned at me and said. "Sometimes he comes. Sometimes he don't."

"That scar on your arm looks like it was a pretty serious stab wound."

"I don't want to talk about that no more," she told me. "That was from a long time ago."

"And you've stuck with him all these years."

She appraised me with those clear blue eyes. "In sickness and in health. I took a vow with my husband."

And then, in an unhappy wave, the realization hit me. My husband had left me for another woman. I turned my face toward the window and whispered, "I understand. I understand why you wouldn't want to be without your husband."

We didn't speak for a while. I was so lost in thought that I nearly forgot the bag lady was even there.

"You're a nice person," the woman suddenly announced. She was studying me again.

I made no reply.

"Do you really think I could do it?" she asked. "Do you think I could leave Larry after all these years?"

I shrugged. "If you want to."

"Lord knows Larry has held me back. I never wanted to end up like this, but I couldn't leave him behind. He needs me to take care of him."

Out the window, the sun was beginning to dip, casting an orange glow over the hills.

"Do it." I leaned toward her. "Start a new life. We can always start brand new. Can't we?"

The woman nodded fervently and I could see a tear escape her eye. She looked around furtively. It was the first time I'd seen her act frightened.

"You're worried about Larry, aren't you? Does he know where you are?"

She nodded. "He always knows where I am."

The train pulled into the Laguna Niguel station and stopped.

"This is your chance," I told her and pointed to the exit. "He's not around. Go."

The woman pursed her lips together in worry and shook her head. After a moment, she rose to her feet, but she was too late. The train took off again.

She sat back down, defeated. Now, it was my turn to stand up.

"What does Larry look like?" I asked her. I planned to make sure he wasn't nearby. Then maybe this woman could make her escape.

"He's tall," she said nervously. "He's big. He's got a red plaid shirt on with a grey T-shirt underneath. His hair is gray, but there's a little black here and there. It's long. You can't miss him because he wears it in a braid down his back. I always loved his long hair!"

She stuck an anguished fist against her mouth and a sob hitched in her throat.

"You deserve to have a decent life," I told her. "You can start over again."

The station of San Juan Capistrano was coming up.

I walked over to the entrance to the next railcar and peered into it. No Larry. There was a staircase that led up to the second level. I climbed the steps and surveyed the area. There were men, but none of them matched Larry's description.

The announcement blared through the train: "Next Stop San Juan Capistrano."

I quickly descended the steps and rounded the corner into our railcar. The bag lady looked at me hopefully.

"He's not around," I told her with some excitement. "Are you going to do it?"

"I am." She wiped away another tear. "I'm going to start over."

I smiled. For weeks I had felt like a trapped animal, pacing behind the bars of the cage of my misery. Helping this woman had given me the most happiness I'd felt in a long while. Perhaps there was hope for me, too.

When the train came to a stop, I walked her to the exit.

"Good luck," I told her.

She hopped off and stood on the platform. She turned to look back at me.

"You're a nice person," she said once more. "You know how to care for people."

I waved to her. She waved back as the doors closed.

I realized then that I never found out her name. I didn't know who she was or where she came from. I wondered where she would go.

Peering into the next car, I half-expected to see a lumberjack of a man come stumbling through, outraged and looking for his wife.

But the train moved along calmly.

I returned to my seat and noticed the bag lady had left her cart.

Oh, poor woman, I thought. Perhaps I could take it to the next station. They might have a Lost and Found and maybe she would think to come for it.

When the train pulled in to the San Clemente station, I tugged the cart out with me. I didn't see a Lost and Found area but I did spot a policeman.

"Excuse me," I asked him. "A homeless lady left her cart on the train. Can you help?"

"Maybe a bag has some identification in it," he offered.

"Probably." I opened the top bag and reached inside. "It's all she has in the world."

I pulled out a red plaid shirt. Feeling a shiver run down my spine, I let it drop to the floor and reached inside again. Out came a grey T-shirt. I held it up like a flag. A large, red-brown stain encircled a two-inch rip in the shirt. The policeman looked at me with renewed interest.

With a pounding heart, I fished deeper into the bag, felt something bristly, and wrapped my fingers around it. Like a rabbit from a magician's top hat, I pulled out a man's skull. I held it by the long black and gray braid still attached to it.

I heard a woman scream. Perhaps it was me. I only know that Larry had never left his wife's side, even after she'd killed him.

And then it hit me with a bang that the witch had gone on to start a new life and left me holding *the bag*!

Sierra Noir
Tim Wohlforth

Fueled by 50 mph winds, the fire swept across the mill town of Sierra. Its citizens rushed to pack family and a few prize possessions in their SUVs and pickups and head out of town before the flames engulfed them. Sirens rent the air. Forest Service fire trucks rolled into town followed by state police and sheriff patrol cars. Local TV reporters showed up and began making live broadcasts from their vans.

The elementary school caught fire. The principal tried to enter his school, but was driven back by heat and smoke. Two churches burned. Midday now appeared as dark as midnight, lit up only by the flames of burning buildings

A lone figure deliberately walked across the town's center square. He wore black jeans and a hoodie, which was tied tightly around his pockmarked face. Cowboy boots. Tall, but so thin that it was a miracle he wasn't swept up with the rest of the flotsam and jetsam. He bent his pencil frame against the winds, while burning branches and ash swirled around him.

He was oblivious to his surroundings, determined to carry out his assigned task. The fire, the smoke, the winds were good cover. She would be driven out of her house to join the hundreds fleeing the town. Then be vulnerable. *There!* He saw a young woman with waist-length straight blond hair emerge from a house on the square. Yes, it was her.

He pulled his 9mm Glock out of his pocket and ran toward her. She saw him. Terror struck her with the force of a blow with rebar. For a critical moment she was paralyzed. That was all the time the killer needed. He fired. She lurched forward. Then he pumped two more bullets into the body. The blond girl collapsed face down in a pile in front of him, hair splayed out over the macadam.

The sound of his gun was lost as the flames reached a large tank at a Suburban Propane station at the other end of the square. It exploded with a flash and a bang that shook the entire town.

The killer wiped off the gun's handle with his jacket's sleeve. As he walked out of town, he tossed the gun near the burning rubble of the Full Gospel Tabernacle.

*

"Our first fatality," Amy Grassy, the town's police chief, said to Lt. John Davis of the California State Police. They stared down at the body of a blond girl sprawled on the pavement in front of them.

"Makes no sense," Amy said. She knelt by the body, but couldn't find a pulse. "Lying out here in the middle of the square. It's not like a burning beam of a building struck her."

Amy was a stocky woman of forty-five, medium height, short straight brown hair. She was tough. She had climbed to the summit of nearby Mt. Shasta over a dozen times, taking four different routes. "Lonely as God and white as a winter moon," they said of the mountain, and it was true. Mt. Shasta was why she had fallen in love with the area and decided to settle here.

Davis said, "Maybe she succumbed to smoke inhalation somewhere else and then staggered out here."

"Maybe," Amy said. Then why, she thought, the blood on her back? She rolled over the body revealing a puddle of blood and what appeared to be three bullet wounds in her gut. "My God! She's been shot."

"I haven't got time for a homicide right now," Davis said. "This whole town's a disaster zone."

"We have to take the time."

"She's your problem. Call it in to Sacramento and ask for a medical examiner and forensic team."

Davis walked back to his patrol car leaving her with the body. *Well, I'm stuck with her,* Amy said to herself. *The way it always works out. The men leave the messes for women to clean up.*

42

She tried to call it in but there was no cell service. The fire had wiped out the tower. She waved down a passing Forest Service SUV. A Ranger—a young woman, so she knew she would get some real help—got her through on her emergency frequency. A lot of good that did her. A male voice told her to "secure the area" until a forensics team arrived.

"How long will that take?"

"A good three to five hours."

"What am I to do in the meantime?"

"Secure the area."

"Are you kidding? We're in the middle of one of the most catastrophic forest fires in years. The town's largely destroyed."

"Sorry about that. Do your best. There are fires everywhere."

She hung up. What a farce.

*

Amy Grassy slumped over her desk in the municipal building, fighting to keep awake. She had hardly slept in the three days since the fire started. She had her patrolmen on overtime as they had battled to prevent looting and keep traffic moving in the cluttered central part of the city. Luckily the municipal building, and therefore her office, being built of brick, hadn't been seriously damaged. A light rain the preceding night had helped dampen the fire, which was now about 60% contained. More than a thousand firemen had taken over a nearby campground. Public Works crews had cleared rubble from the town square.

She knew it was time to start work on the homicide of the blond girl. The medical examiner and the forensics team had come and gone. Their reports had yielded little that wasn't obvious to John Davis and her when they had discovered the body. Died from three gun wounds pumped into her at close range—9mm rounds.

Amy had gotten one break. One of her officers attended the Full Gospel Tabernacle. A parishioner had discovered a Glock pistol near the wreckage of the charred sanctuary and turned it over to him. Amy sent it to Sacramento to see if it was a match for the bullets retrieved from the young woman's body. She hadn't heard yet, but assumed that there would be. Which wouldn't be a hell of a lot of help as the weapon had been wiped clean of fingerprints, and its serial number had been filed off. It was possible, Sacramento told her, to raise filed-off serial numbers, but this required costly work. At her department's expense. She had told them to go ahead. She'd bury the cost in the overruns that resulted from the fire. She was told not to expect results in less than two weeks.

The body had been identified as belonging to a Cherry Watson, nineteen years old, who worked as a bookkeeper at the mill. Moved up here six months ago from LA. The family was preparing to have the body shipped down south for a memorial service and a burial. That is, once she had released it. Which she hadn't yet. It was presently residing in the morgue at the local hospital. She hesitated. Why? She wasn't sure, but she couldn't stall much longer.

So, exhausted as she was, Amy forced her tired ass out of her chair and into her patrol car. She needed to take a trip to the mill. She had an appointment with Sam Hicks, its owner, and George Williams of Cal Fire.

*

Amy drove through the disaster zone that had once been the town she loved so much. She passed empty foundations and skeletal remains of the homes that belonged to the Edwards family, the Chavezes, the O'Reillys—all gray and lifeless. A touch of red from a toy truck, a green tricycle, indicated the once vigorous life of her adopted home. Here and there she spotted a yellow-clad fireman dousing a hot spot. The occupants of these homes were now staying with relatives or in motels in nearby communities. But they would return. Yes, her people would rebuild, her town would survive.

She slowed as she approached the massive plywood and composite board mill. It stretched a quarter-mile along a ridge slightly above the town. It usually spouted exhaust and fumes from the glue used in the manufacturing process. A hub of activity with trucks unloading timber and huge forklifts moving slabs of plywood to flatbed rail cars. Today it was ghastly and ghostly still. Not even wind blowing.

She spotted thin wisps of smoke coming from what was once the front office. Two trucks from Cal Fire stood by the entrance. Firemen blasted water on the remains of a smoldering fire. Amy braked, turned off her engine, and jumped out of the patrol car. No sense getting too close. You never know when these things can suddenly flare up. She was assaulted by a blast of acrid air. Her eyes watered and she wanted to flee back into her car and get the hell out of there. But she had a job to do.

Ahead she spotted Hicks' black BMW with Williams' bright red SUV pulled next to it. Both men stood in front of the mill and were engaged in a heated exchange. Amy recognized the tall, muscular, handsome man in running sweats as Hicks. She had a history with that man, and not a pleasant one. In her opinion he cared nothing for the town and the people who worked in his mill. He pushed production at the price of safety. A friend of hers in the Forest Service said he was fudging on his report of timber cut. But he couldn't prove it and upper management was not interested in pursuing the matter. The short gray-haired roly-poly guy must be Williams of Cal Fire. The two stopped talking as she approached.

"Thank you, Chief, for joining us," Williams said. He was the one in charge, the wealthy Hicks reduced to a supplicant.

"How can I help you?" Amy asked.

"Our investigators say the fire began around noon right here in this office, and then spread, fueled by the 50 mph winds. I've been questioning Mr. Hicks on how that could've happened. It appears to be a mystery to him."

Hicks answered, "Williams claims the fire was deliberately set." The guy was smooth, always in control of his emotions. Yet this time Amy spotted a slight tick in his face. Yes, he was nervous, very nervous.

"We've found no evidence of an accelerant being used," Williams said. "It's possible that the cause was faulty wiring. There's little left of the structure to tell. However, there's one peculiar feature. We found a deeply scorched wastebasket in the accounting office. Were you, by any chance, burning some papers there and the flames got away from you?"

"Not a chance. Why would I be doing that? Actually at the time I was addressing a Rotary meeting in Yreka on environmentally sustainable timber harvesting."

Amy asked, "Who was left in charge of the office?"

"The foremen were out in the plant," Hicks said. "Only one person was in the office, the bookkeeper Cherry Watson."

"Maybe she could've been burning something," Williams said. "However she's in no condition to answer our questions, as she was shot under mysterious circumstances the afternoon of the fire. Could her death have any connection to her work at your mill?"

"I've no idea who shot Miss Watson or why. Perhaps a jealous boyfriend. She was quite pretty. I understand she had a habit of partying in town after work."

Now Amy was pissed. Typical of a man to blame the victim. Happens all the time in rape cases. But this is murder. She wouldn't let him get away with it.

She said, "She had no steady boyfriend. Her friends in town say she was a quiet person and spent most of her spare time pursuing an online a BA in preparation for a CPA exam."

Hicks turned away from them and prepared to get back in his car. Amy, addressing his back, said, "I have one more question, Mr. Hicks, if you don't mind. Why did you deposit $5,000 in Cherry's bank account the week before the fire?"

Hicks swung around and glared at her. He wasn't used to being questioned by someone he considered subordinate to him.

"What're you implying? She asked me for an advance on her salary and I gave it to her. Cherry told me she wanted to buy a small fixer-upper and needed money for the down payment. If you have any more questions please call my lawyer."

He turned away from her, entered his car, started up the engine.

"We'll be in touch," Amy shouted after him. "My investigation has only just begun."

Hicks sped off, but she knew he had heard her.

Williams asked her, "What do you make of it?"

"I suspect Hicks was cheating the Forest Service. I understand some of his timber harvesting reports are suspiciously low. Cherry caught him at it. He paid her off to keep her quiet and to burn the evidence. Then had her killed to be on the safe side."

"And the fire that wiped out most of the town?"

"I don't think either of them expected the wastebasket fire to get out of control. No one was prepared for the horrific wind that blew through the town the night of the wildfire."

"That's all speculation."

"For now, yes. But I've just got started."

"Be careful," Williams said to her.

"What do you mean?"

"Hicks has a lot of clout. This town is dependent on him. He has friends high up in the Forest Service. His plant is on land leased from the Service and most of the logs milled here are from Sierra Timber, which pays millions to the Service. And if you're right that he paid to have Cherry killed, he might be willing to pay again to remove you. Your reputation for being dogged is well known throughout this mountain country."

"And what are you going to do?"

"I'm going to submit my report to the higher-ups in the Service."

"And what are they going to do?"

"Don't hold your breath on that one. Best to just go on with your life. We're both out of our league."

But Amy wasn't built to just go on with her life. That's not why she became a cop. Justice was her life.

*

A solitary figure, dressed in black jeans and hoodie, crossed the deserted town center of Sierra the next night. It was 3 a.m. and pitch black. The streetlights had yet to be repaired. From time to time he turned on a pocket-sized Maglite to get his bearings. He crossed the square and headed up Maple Street, then Pine to find the address he had been given by his employer.

The hooded man's target lived in a two-story redwood house that had been spared by the fire. He pried open a back window, crawled in and found himself in the kitchen. He flashed on his light for a brief second and saw a door that led to the rest of the house. Passing through the portal, the intruder came to stairs leading to a second floor. He silently crept up the stairs, entered the open door of a bedroom and stood for a minute to allow his eyes to adjust to the darkness. The intruder could barely make out a bed and a large mound in its center.

The figure approached the bed intent on suffocating the sleeping occupant. He grabbed a pillow and flung himself down on the mound.

Bright light blasted the room. Amy, in her pajamas, hovered over him, holding a Smith & Wesson 9mm pistol. He turned, twisted smile on his face. As if he didn't mind getting caught. He was counting on Hicks' high-priced lawyers. Might even get a bonus.

She said, "Now let's have a little discussion."

Silence.

"We can begin with your name. Then, more importantly, the name of your employer."

Silence.

"It's Hicks, right?"

Silence.

"You're aware I can shoot you as an intruder."

Silence.

She moved closer to him and began to squeeze the trigger.

The intruder rushed her, trying to wrench the gun out of her hand. She blocked his move, grabbed his arm, bent down and flung him over her shoulder. He cried out as he landed on his back. The first sound he had made since she confronted him in her bedroom.

It would be his last. She pulled the trigger on her gun.

Bang! Bang! Bang! Bang! The shots reverberated throughout the room, breaking the still of the Sierra night. In the distance an owl hooted.

She lay down her gun and felt for his pulse. None. Checked his pockets for identification. Nothing. Picking up her cell phone from the bed stand, she speed-dialed the police station. Patrolman Allen Stagway would be on night duty.

"Allen, better come on over to my place. Been an intruder. I've shot him."

"Should I contact EMT?"

"No need. He's dead. Call the Sheriff and the State Police."

Amy hung up. She looked forward to a decent night's sleep. This bastard had caused her to lose sleep two nights in a row.

I've got one of 'em.

So far.

Thor's Breath
Suzanne Berube Rorhus

Hamarr caught himself whistling as he unlatched the cover of the mechanism that powered the oars of Chief Trygve's longboat. He glanced around to see if anyone had noticed, but he was alone at the edge of the fjord. Bad enough his occupation was considered women's work, he didn't need to be caught whistling like a little girl as well.

He wrestled the huge boiler to one side, his biceps straining against the sleeves of his tunic. Once the boiler was out of the way, he could examine the workings of the steam engine. He stood, stretching a kink out of his back. He wiped his greasy hands on his breeches, then secured his thick blond hair with a leather thong to keep it from the engine's moving parts.

Hamarr was the only mechanical healer in this remote coastal area of Norway in the year of that Christian Lord 627. As such, Hamarr was responsible for ensuring the region's steam engines did their work, despite the evil spirits that were determined to bedevil all mechanical things.

Magic and healing were traditionally practiced by women in Viking society, while the men focused on the more traditional skills of farming and raiding. Vikings were happy enough when their women were as fierce and independent as men, but significantly less pleased when men were careful and clever as women.

Today, he had to mend a flaw in the chief's longboat. The village men had planned on beginning a sea voyage to the northwest coast of the Frankish lands today to raid the towns and monasteries of their gold and wine, but the voyage had been delayed by a malicious spirit in the engine that drove the oars.

After examining the engine's components, Hamarr discovered a frayed leather belt. Once he replaced it, the gears would again dip and pull the oars in unison, conveying the warriors on their voyage. Hamarr, for one, couldn't wait to see them leave.

He preferred his village with the warriors gone. Now that the summer season had arrived with its nearly perpetual sunshine, it was time for the raids and trading trips that allowed the village to thrive during the dark winter months. With the warriors gone, Hamarr would be able to work in peace, creating and repairing the machines the women used for farming in the men's absence. If time permitted, he would also work on his inventions. He'd received a black powder from the Orient that he was most eager to explore.

"And have you finished yet?" a voice boomed. Hamarr jerked his head around. Chief Trygve had joined him in the boat's hull, sneaking up on leather-covered feet.

"I have. Shall we take her out for a test?" Hamarr gazed directly into the eyes of his chief. He'd learned to meet a man's eyes. If he left his gaze on his mechanical treasures as he preferred, other men took that as a sign of weakness. Machines and their magic were not worthy of a grown man's attention.

Hamarr loved the machines, though he would never admit to such a thing. The interaction of the endless gears and belts, driven by the steam from the boilers, could accomplish so much more than a man alone.

Hamarr reconnected the engine's components as the chief watched, then shoved the boiler back into position. He stoked the fire with a few armfuls of coal, fanning the flames until the temperature within grew hot enough to produce the needed steam. Satisfied, Hamarr untied the dragon ship from its mooring and pushed it away from shore.

He led Chief Trygve to the stern. Hamarr had installed a new starter for the oars' engine, allowing the apparatus to be controlled from the wheelhouse rather than the hull.

"One push here," he said, demonstrating by poking a wooden knob, "and the boiler will release steam into the apparatus. This will drive the oars in unison, propelling the boat forward."

The engine banged then roared into life, frightening a flock of puffins into flight. Steam hissed and rattled before escaping through the opening in the ship's dragon figurehead. The dragon's mouth now emitted the steamy breath that so frightened their foes. The oars swung in unison above the water.

"Spare me the magic lesson," the chief said. "Will she get us to the Frankish lands? I won't have my men stranded on the seas with nothing to drive the oars."

Hamarr jerked the lever to lower the oars into the sea and the boat lurched forward. "She'll get you to the Frankish lands easily enough, though you will need to refill your charcoal stores to return home."

Eventually satisfied, the chief returned to the quay and allowed Hamarr to tie up the boat and shut down the apparatus. The men would depart on the morrow.

Hamarr untied his mechanical dog Hellshund from the tree where he'd left him and walked home. Hellshund, his head as high as Hamarr's belt, growled joyfully as steam issued from his nose.

When Hamarr arrived home, his wife and children greeted him at the door. His youngest son clambered aboard Hellshund, riding the dog as if it were a pony. Hellshund sneezed, scalding the ankle of Hamarr's eldest daughter with a stream of boiling water as she set the evening meal on the table. She yelped and kicked at the dog, but Hellshund easily dodged the blow.

Hamarr sat down to his meal. He'd received a hare from yesterday's labors on the lathe at the Larson farm, so tonight they supped on rabbit fricassee and boiled kohlrabi. After dinner, he lounged on a fur-covered bench as his children played a complicated game with stones and twigs, and his wife wove cloth on her loom. Steam belched from the loom as she worked, and Hamarr fell asleep to the comforting, repetitive sound.

Midmorning, Hamarr called in at the blacksmith, Kjetil, who slapped Hamarr on the back. "You missed quite the drinks party last night. The men were eager for their mead and the women were eager for their men."

Kjetil, now in his fifties, no longer participated in the raids, but Hamarr suspected he missed the excitement. Though twice Hamarr's age, the men had bonded over their mutual interest in things mechanical. "I passed a quiet night in my bed," Hamarr said. "I suppose you woke with a sore head today, though, did you not?"

"That I did. But the warriors are gone now and we have our time to ourselves. You said you received a new material from the Far East? When will you show it to me?"

"Now." Hamarr reached into his tunic and removed a square of cloth tied into a bundle. He set the bundle on Kjetil's work bench and gently untied the thong. The cloth fell open, revealing a mound of black powder. "I have a barrel of this, for which I traded more gold than I'd like to admit."

Kjetil poked the powder with his finger. "What is it?" He brought his finger to his lips and touched his tongue, grimacing at the bitter taste.

"Those in the Orient call it fire medicine. They use this powder to make stones fly like arrows."

Kjetil scoffed. "It takes a catapult to make a stone fly. You were suckered out of your gold."

"We'll see."

Hellshund sneezed at that moment, launching a small hot coal through his nostrils. The coal landed on the black powder, resulting in a huge explosion for such a tiny pile.

Hamarr laughed at Kjetil's expression. "You see the possibilities, my friend? There is indeed fire locked inside this powder."

Shaken, Kjetil could only nod.

They passed ten days exploring the black powder. When they threw a handful into the flames of Kjetil's forge, the powder flashed and burned unusually hot. When Kjetil struck a pile of powder placed on his anvil, the powder exploded and caught fire.

"It's a wondrous substance," Kjetil admitted as the two men drank mead in front of Kjetil's hearth. An Irish slave girl served them venison roasted over the spit. As she placed the wooden platter at Kjetil's side, he reached out to pat her bottom. "Aileen here is a pretty thing, is she not? Dumb as a bag of hammers, though. She can't understand even simple speech."

"You have had her for more than a year, have you not?" Hamarr said. "She should have learned to speak by now, savage though she may be."

"Eh, she probably fakes her ignorance. I bought her last year after the raid upon Dublin. She keeps my bed warm at least, now that Torhilda has joined her ancestors."

Hamarr dismissed the inconsequential plight of a slave with a wave of his hand. "Let's figure out a use for this powder. I want to have something to present to Chief Trygve upon his return. If we have nothing new, we will not receive our shares of the raid's proceeds."

"If we are to please the chief, we need to fashion the powder into a weapon." Kjetil stroked the back of his own mechanical dog, a beast nearly as large as Hellshund. "A magic as powerful as this can conquer the world."

"If we have to get close enough to our enemies to sprinkle them with powder, we are unlikely to survive the encounter," Hamarr mused. "We need a way to send the powder some distance. Perhaps a catapult, as you suggested."

They tinkered with the fire medicine for a couple more weeks, whenever they could steal time from their duties.

Their work was interrupted one night by the arrival of a slave from another farm. Kjetil pointed him out to Hamarr when he spotted the youth skulking into his yard. "That one is brother to my own Aileen," he said. "Come. Let us see why he is disturbing her in her labors."

When they entered Kjetil's home, the two Irish slaves were chattering in their own incomprehensible language. "Something's not right," Kjetil whispered to Hamarr. "This is the first time the girl has smiled since she arrived. What are they up to?"

"What can a slave be up to?" Hamarr asked. "Let's go. We have work to do."

The breakthrough happened one night when Hamarr was alone. He'd been sitting on a log in the woods after a hunting trip, warming his hands in the steamy breath of Hellshund. The dog sneezed, scorching Hamarr's hands with a pellet of coal.

Hamarr patted the dog. "That's it, Hellshund! We shall use your steam to propel this fire medicine."

He led the dog to Kjetil's workshop and the two men worked feverishly for several days. Hamarr added pine resin to the fire medicine to allow it to burn longer. Interestingly, this created a liquid fire that clung to all it touched. When he added a trace of quicksilver, even water could not extinguish the flames. The two men burned Kjetil's storage shed to the ground the first time they tried this combination, but so jubilant were they that Kjetil did not mind the loss of the outbuilding.

Hamarr named the new substance Thor's Breath. He had Hellshund's chest open and was digging in its depths. "Look, Kjetil. If I add an earthenware pot here, Hellshund can carry the liquid fire in his gut. Then, using steam, he can launch Thor's Breath from a pewter spigot in his mouth and light it from the fire of his breath."

Kjetil continued Hamarr's thought. "And if it works in the dogs, we can place it into the figurehead of the raiding boat just as easily."

Hamarr laughed. "But instead of steam coming from the dragon's mouth, it will be fire!"

Aileen brought them a cold supper and two flagons of mead. She grinned as she placed their meal on the workbench.

"She's making me crazy," Kjetil said to his friend. "She smiles. And she sings. I think she and her brother are plotting something."

"What will they do? Walk to Ireland? You worry too much. Let us focus. I want to create a prototype before the warriors return."

"You know," Kjetil said, "We could sell this for tons of gold. The Orient may pay for the improvements we've made to their black powder. Or the Greeks! The Greeks are always looking for new weapons."

"You want to sell liquid fire to the Greeks? That's a horrible idea. They'd just try to use it against us."

"Hmm. Perhaps."

The next morning they began construction on the dogs' new innards. While Kjetil created the earthenware bladders and the spigots for the two dogs, Hamarr worked out the details of the program for the dogs to follow. After only ten days, Hamarr was satisfied with their work.

"This should do it," he said to Kjetil. "All we need is to test it."

"I cannot offer my storage shed, I'm afraid," Kjetil said, "since it is already in ashes."

As it turned out, they did not need a building on which to test Thor's Breath.

They were strolling through the forest, trailed by the two hounds, when Aileen and her brother ran past.

The men followed the youths toward the shore, mechanical dogs hissing and clanging behind them. The Irish boy turned to look at them, then pointed out into the fjord.

On the horizon, a small warship sailed toward the village. As they watched it approach, the boy said, "My father is Irish chief. We go home now."

Kjetil grabbed Aileen by her arm. The brother swung at Kjetil, striking the older man in the jaw before Hamarr could react. Aileen took advantage of his surprise to wriggle free. She ran to the dock, followed by her brother. Hamarr helped Kjetil to his feet, steadying the dazed man.

By now Aileen and her brother were on the village dock, waving frantically to the ship as it approached.

"Don't let them get away," Kjetil demanded, rubbing his sore jaw. "I will have that boy's head on a stake by the end of the day."

"More importantly, if those Irish warriors invade the village while the raiders are away, they will find it easy pickings," Hamarr said, pointing at the ship now dockside. Fierce men in full battle armament lined the ship's side, helping the two Irish youth board.

Kjetil swore. "We need to warn the village. Send one of the dogs for help."

"We need them," Hamarr said. "Gather them by the shore. Maybe Thor's Breath can repel those warriors."

Together they propelled the dogs to the dock just as the first of the Irishmen climbed from the warship. This man, tall and strong with fiery red hair and beard, was clearly the chieftain, for all the Irishmen looked to him for direction. The man paused, assessing Hamarr and Kjetil and their dogs.

"I wager these barbarians have never seen a mechanical dog," Hamarr said. He and Kjetil flung coal from their knapsacks into the bellies of the hounds as quickly as they could, stoking their fires higher.

Hamarr slammed the coal bins closed. He pulled the levers, first on Hellshund, then on Kjetil's dog, freeing the flow of Thor's Breath to the dogs' maws. On his command, the dogs stepped onto the wooden dock.

The chieftain spouted orders in his native tongue and Irishmen disembarked the warship, lining up in front of their ship, weapons at the ready. In moments, the entire band would be ashore.

"Fire!" Kjetil shouted.

"I don't know if it's ready," Hamarr complained. "We haven't even tested the propulsion."

"Unless you wish to become an Irish slave, fire!"

With a muttered curse, Hamarr engaged the mechanism and pressed the control button on Hellshund.

Thor's Breath spurted out, ignited by Hellshund's breath. He did the same with Kjetil's dog with the same results. Instead of a long stream of burning liquid, the dogs only managed a weak spit and drool.

The chieftain and his men backed up closer to their ship but they did not yet abandon the fight.

"You need more propulsion if you are going to reach the ship. Fire again!" Kjetil said.

Unfortunately, neither dog managed to propel Thor's Breath more than five feet. From their position at the land's edge, they were not able to reach the Irishmen with the Thor's Breath. They did, however, manage to set fire to the dock. The flames, fanned by the sea breeze, advanced on the Irishmen until they were forced to reboard their ship. The ship pushed away from shore as the last of the dock burned into the water.

"At least they can't invade us without getting their feet wet," Hamarr said. The two men continued to add coal to the dogs, trying to build up enough heat to propel Thor's Breath onto the warship.

At long last, the chieftain seemed to give up in disgust. He waved a fist at Hamarr and Kjetil and shouted what must have been curses in his language. Then, turning to his crew, he gave an order and the ship set a course back to Ireland.

Hamarr and Kjetil deconstructed the event over mead and roasted pigeon by Hamarr's fire that evening. The youngest son sat on his father's knee, playing with his beard as the men spoke.

"We have failed," Hamarr said. "We needed Thor's Breath to spew with the strength of a waterfall, and instead it bubbled with the force of a drooling infant."

Kjetil gestured at Hamarr's son. "Is your boy a slave on an Irish ship? No, he is not. We did not fail. We discouraged the attackers who would rape our women and steal our children. We just need to tweak a few details."

"You made an interesting point earlier," Hamarr said, "about sending one of the dogs for help. If we could work out a way to use steam to send messages over long distances, that would be useful indeed."

Kjetil scoffed. "That will never happen." He waved the leg of his roasted pigeon. "You might as well ask the birds to carry messages for us."

Hamarr laughed. "Perhaps you are right. So, what do you think Chief Trygve will give us when he sees Thor's Breath?"

"I want a new slave," Kjetil said. "And she'd better be beautiful and strong."

"And not the daughter of a chieftain," Hamarr agreed.

Arthur

Sandra Murphy

"Arthur, knock it off. Popcorn farts are the worst." Debbie left with the bowl, like that would do any good. I'd already eaten my fill. Mostly.

In a minute, she was back, spritzing clouds of air freshener, which made me sneeze. "Sleep on the couch. We've got Detweiller's tomorrow. I need my rest." Like I cared. A comfy couch and an afghan to keep me warm. Ha! There's dropped popcorn under the table—five-minute rule!

*

Debbie and I disagree about the car. I don't drive and there are times I think she shouldn't either. The way she takes a turn would make anybody a little sick. I like fresh air; she likes the heat on high. We had our usual argument about that, but since I'd held back a few popcorn farts, I won.

We arrived at Detweiller Industries twenty minutes later. It might have taken fifteen, if I hadn't gotten into a bit of a shouting match with a pint-sized big mouth in the next car at a red light. Debbie tried to be the peace maker. She should have had my back, no matter who was right, which of course, was me. But I digress.

Usually, we see the receptionist, the security guy, a secretary or three and a few assorted minions, but today, the big man himself met us at the door. Ted's nothing special, taller than Debbie but only a little. not by much. That's balanced out by outweighing her by a hundred pounds, not much of it hair, most of it stomach and tush. Ted worries a lot and I would guess, nervous eating is his way of handling stress.

As best I can figure, and I admit I don't pay a lot of attention to details, Detweiller makes stuff for the government. Ted's employees have to be trustworthy, and most of all, sober. That's where I come in. I'm the drug tester.

Let me give you my credentials. Usually, I'm called Artie, but when annoyed, Debbie calls me Arthur. Come to think of it, she does that a lot. My full name is Arthur T. Terrier. T for Trouble, and Trouble's my middle name! Terrier is my dad's name. He's John Russell Terrier, Jack for short. That's where I get my tenacity. Mom is distantly related to Bloodhounds. That's where I get my super-sniffer, some forty-five times better than a human's puny nose. My small stature allows me to tunnel under, climb over and search places no one, except the bad guy, would think of going.

My training was expensive from what I hear, but I don't really deal with cash, you know? The first two jobs I had, well, they didn't go so great. I'm not the best fit for corporate life. There's no room for thinking outside the box, where, if you want to know, a guy like me finds the most drugs. Debbie and I are partners. It works as long as she listens to me.

On the way to the plant, we saw Greg, the janitor, in the lobby. He wiped his runny nose, scratched himself (Debbie says I shouldn't scratch there when we're out in public) and dumped a bunch of gray water on the floor to mop. I wouldn't have wanted to be Greg if it had gotten on Debbie's new suede boots, the ones with only a couple of bite marks that show.

In the plant, Debbie took off my leash and told me, "Find it!" I love that part! Boy, did I ever find it. There was a stash under the big machine. People seem to think that the smell of machine oil and general crud hide the odor of marijuana, but it doesn't—not from me. I did a perfect point so Debbie could see the hide. I found more back where they cut the wood for pallets. In the bathroom, the smell of orange was strong, but not as strong as the old nose. I've got to say, I did a stellar job.

We ended up in Ted's office, a rare thing. Ted droned on about a leak and the computer. Frankly, I don't get computers except YouTube. There's a video of this one bitch...but I digress. I tuned out most of what he said and caught a few zzzs.

On the way out, Debbie talked to herself. I could tell because she didn't say Artie first. It was about who could have access to the computers. Plant employees would be too noticeable. Maybe security? Ted's secretary, a nice lady with dog biscuits in the desk drawer, the third one on the left, couldn't be the one. (I don't eat on the job so she always gives me a to-go bag.)

Debbie rambled on but I'd caught The Smell. I went into Stealth Mode, and for once, Debbie noticed right away. Ahead of us in the hall was Greg, running the thing that swirls around and makes the floor shiny and good for a running slide, if one is not held back by the other end of the leash. I knew I'd have to show Debbie instead of just pointing so I ran as fast as I could (that's real fast), jumped up and bit Greg on the butt! It was stellar I tell you! I tore his coveralls and eww, there was his hairy old butt hanging out, all wrinkly. The swirly machine went wild until security pulled the plug.

Janitors can be anywhere without being questioned or even noticed—except by Yours Truly, who sniffed out the cocaine in his back pocket. Some gizmo called a flash drive hit the floor and Debbie got all excited. Turns out, Greg was Gregor, a Russian, sending information to the Old Country.

Ted was pleased, we got a raise...and me? I got more popcorn! Debbie sat in the recliner and pointed the fan in my direction.

Debbie said she's calling this The Case of the Flashing Butt.

Fractured Memories
Julie Tollefson

Keith clamped his jaws together. The inside of his mouth crackled as the dried sugary residue that coated his mucous membranes shattered into tiny shards like broken glass.

Good lord, how much bourbon and Coke did he drink last night? He had the massive headache that in his younger days meant he'd had a helluva good time. Today, it just meant he'd survived another of Andrea's legendary Fourth of July parties.

He pushed himself into a sitting position, then fell back against the sofa cushions when nausea threatened. He'd passed out on the sofa, head tilted back, mouth wide open. Thus, the crackle mouth. Whatever he'd done, Andrea must have been pissed to leave him here like this. She was usually such a stickler for sleeping in the same bed every night, no matter what.

He closed his eyes. A kaleidoscope of dizzying images from the party flashed against his eyelids in harsh, red-tinged colors. Tanks and rockets and things Keith couldn't identify that buzzed and jumped and sparked and popped. He opened his eyes again before the images made him sick.

Andrea loved fireworks with the passion of a ten-year-old girl. Their Fourth of July party had grown over the years from a few close friends chucking firecrackers at tin cans and knocking back cheap beer, to a few dozen acquaintances indulging in ever more impressive pyrotechnic displays and ever-more-expensive booze.

A thud shook the floor and roused Keith from the sofa. He traced the string of curses that followed to the kitchen and Andrea's biggest client, Barry Larson. Barry's long arms draped atop the refrigerator's wide-open double doors. He hung his head inside, another party casualty.

"Epic party, Keith."

That Barry, a thirty-eight-year-old professional who craved all the finer things money could buy, chose to talk like he imagined an unemployed twenty-year-old surfer would irritated Keith as much as the knowledge that without Barry's business, Andrea would lose hers. He was one of her first clients and three years later was still her most lucrative. That didn't mean Keith had to like him.

Past Barry, the window above the sink perfectly framed the backyard destruction. Singed paper confetti, plastic rockets, cardboard mortar tubes. A parachute swung from the rain gutter. Andrea's "launch pad," a piece of plywood balanced on two saw horses, had fallen askew, a hole the size of Keith's fist burned in the middle where she'd lit her massive nightworks display.

How much did you spend this year?

Don't be such a spoilsport, Keith.

I thought you'd grow out of it by now.

Grow out of patriotism?

Keith snorted. Patriotism had nothing to do with his wife's addiction to the flash and the bang.

"Coffee, man. You guys have some, right? I need caffeine like whoa."

Barry rifled through the cabinet to Keith's left, the smell of stale beer and cheese dip on his breath strong enough to drive Keith back against the opposite counter. A pyramid of soda cans toppled and clattered down beside two bourbon bottles—the cheap stuff he bought for parties and the good stuff he reserved for himself—both empty.

As the last can hit the floor, the door to the guest room swung open and Andrea's best friend, Tiffany Glen, emerged, disheveled and green. Keith looked from her to Barry and back again. It appeared their party had entered new territory: facilitating hookups between Andrea's business partner and one of their biggest clients.

Tiffany caught his eye and shrugged.

A thick shroud of post-party gloom sucked the air from the kitchen. Keith left Barry and Tiffany to their hangovers and regrets and stumbled to the door. Fresh air would help him clear his head, if not the fuzzy coating on his tongue and the taste of bile at the back of his throat. Maybe by the time he returned, Barry and Tiffany would be gone.

The stench of smoke and gunpowder assaulted him as soon as he stepped out the back door. He sidestepped the beer bottles and paper plates that littered the porch and dragged a trash can toward Andrea's launch pad. Cleanup. His party specialty.

Through the burned-out hole in the middle of the launch pad, Keith glimpsed a jumble of cardboard boxes, plastic wraps, and depleted artillery shells. He moved the ruined plywood aside.

And discovered his wife, half covered by the remains of the fireworks she loved, a gaping bloody hole in her chest.

Keith stumbled to the edge of the woods and vomited beside his favorite redbud tree.

*

Reality played tricks on Keith.

Tiffany appeared at his side, her mouth an *O* of shock and disbelief.

Barry attempted to embrace him in a clumsy one-armed man hug.

A wind-whipped parachute landed on his foot.

The backyard filled with strangers in uniform while he cradled his wife's body close to his chest.

"Mr. Walton?"

A gray-haired cop in a suit put a hand on Keith's shoulder. He'd been speaking for some time, Keith realized.

"I'm sorry. I…"

The cop—detective, he supposed, because of the suit—led him toward the house and into his library, where he sat stiff-backed in one of the black leather barrel chairs that flanked the fireplace. Someone put a glass of water in his hand. Someone else pulled the shades, plunging the room into darkness and blocking his view of the backyard.

Andrea was dead. How? Keith searched his bourbon-broken memories. Hot artichoke dip bubbling in the oven. Bunting and flags on the front porch. The dining room table laden with chips and dips, olives, red-white-and-blue cake.

"Mr. Walton?" The gray-haired detective sat in the opposite chair, notebook open on his lap. "What time did the party break up?"

Keith rubbed his temples. He hadn't felt this alcohol-sick in a decade.

"I came inside at dusk, I think. Andrea and her friends were about to light the nightworks. She's usually so careful. I don't understand how this could happen."

"*Her* friends?"

"Our friends, I guess."

The detective wrote in his notebook. The library smelled sweet-sour, of sweat and alcohol and leather. The low table in front of the sofa held two rocks glasses and another half-empty bottle of bourbon, a rare, handcrafted brand. A contribution from one of Andrea's wealthy clients, no doubt.

"You didn't watch the fireworks?" The detective kept his tone neutral but Keith felt the jab just the same.

"My wife says I worry too much. I imagine the worst."

"The worst."

"Fingers blown off, burns, that kind of thing. I never imagined… How did…? What kind…?" He didn't know how to ask which one of Andrea's beloved fireworks killed her. The explosive must have malfunctioned, to hit her squarely in the chest.

The detective rose and pulled aside the curtain on the window that overlooked the backyard. He stared outside for a long minute, then turned back to Keith.

"You came in here for a drink?"

Keith nodded slowly. He must have. The proof was on the table.

"Who drank from the other glass?"

Keith had been trying to pull that fragment from the shattered remnants of his memories since he saw the second glass. Nothing surfaced.

The detective raised one eyebrow a fraction of a centimeter.

"I…" Keith snapped his mouth shut. He couldn't say that he didn't have an explanation, that none of the guests would have joined him in here when the action was outside, that the library was his personal sanctuary where he retreated, alone, to avoid the crowds of people who were not really his friends because he never made the effort to be friendly.

The sourness of the room suffocated him.

"That's my glass, detective."

Tiffany stood just inside the open door, her hands wrapped tightly around a twisted piece of bunting. Her knuckles glowed white against the red-and-blue plastic decoration.

The detective looked from Keith to Tiffany and back. Keith squeezed his eyes shut against the suspicions he saw plainly written on the detective's face. But when he opened them again, nothing had changed.

She curled onto the sofa, feet tucked under and head in hand. "You were already pretty far gone when I came inside, Keith."

Her voice held a note of something intimate and secret. It turned Keith's stomach.

He slouched in his chair and struggled to make sense out of the senseless. Andrea was dead. Dead. He saw again the hole in her chest. And the two empty glasses beside the bottle of bourbon. He raked trembling fingers through his hair. Why couldn't he remember what happened last night?

Barry stumbled into the library and plopped onto the sofa beside Tiffany. Annoyance flickered across the detective's face, but a more interesting emotion arced between Andrea's number one client and her business partner—anxiety tinged with lust.

The detective folded his notebook closed. "I'll need a list of your guests, Mr. Walton."

"I don't understand. Why didn't anyone call for help? There must have been thirty people here last night."

"For god's sake, Keith." Tiffany broke in. "Isn't it obvious? Andrea didn't have an accident. Somebody killed her."

Her words hit Keith in the gut.

"You mean accidentally," he said. "Carelessness or..."

His voice trailed off. The detective stared hard at him, judging his reaction, but he was past reacting.

*

The three of them—Keith, Tiffany and Barry—sat together at the kitchen table under the watchful eye of a uniformed officer while the detective supervised a search of the house.

"Dude, this is messed up," Barry said. He drummed nervously on the table, faster and faster until Keith thought the table would shake apart.

Tiffany lit a cigarette, something she never would have done when Andrea was alive. Keith watched the smoke rise toward the ceiling. He felt his indifference as an affront to his dead wife's memory.

"What happened to you, Keith? You used to love this as much as I do."

He couldn't tell her it had all been a lie, an illusion he'd created to make his youthful self more interesting to her. In the two decades since they'd married, the effort of maintaining the illusion became too much under the weight of adult responsibilities.

When had he last talked to his wife? Really talked? He almost smiled when he remembered. Sunday, over brunch. He'd ordered tomato juice. She ordered a mimosa. He considered every item on the menu before settling for his usual, two poached eggs on toast. She ordered the special without even asking what it was. A metaphor for their life together. Keith, measured and steady. Dull. Andrea, passionate and daring.

Only they hadn't really talked, had they? *She* had talked, while he read the business section of the Sunday paper, muttering "yes" and "I see" when it seemed appropriate. Now, with his wife murdered, his guilt gave that last one-sided conversation an outsized importance. He pulled at his hair as he tried to remember.

He'd put the paper down when his eggs came. By then, she'd fallen uncharacteristically silent. She barely touched her banana bread French toast drizzled with chocolate raspberry cream. He had the feeling he'd missed something significant.

"What does Tiffany say?"

He remembered asking the question. She had paused, mimosa halfway to her lips, and scowled.

"You haven't been listening. It's all about money to her."

"Maybe she's right."

"You wouldn't understand."

The detective emerged from the library and for the second time that morning, Keith's utterly predictable world shifted on its axis. The detective held a gun in his gloved hand. Andrea's gun, which she always kept locked in the gun safe in the basement.

Tiffany's eyes darted from the gun to Keith to Barry, then settled on Keith.

"My god, Keith."

Blood rushed to his face as all three of them stared at him. Another wave of nausea slammed over him at the realization that they all thought *he'd* killed his wife.

Barry shook his head sadly. "Dude."

*

Keith felt trapped. For a fleeting moment, he imagined giving in to his desire to run from the kitchen and keep running. How far would he get before one of the cops brought him down? And how guilty would he look?

"What happened last night, Mr. Walton?" The detective handed the gun to a uniformed officer.

For the first time in years, Keith wished he'd stayed at Andrea's side for the duration of the party. If he had been with her, if he'd stopped after one glass of bourbon, if he hadn't sequestered himself in the library. If. If. If.

"Next year will be different. Just a few friends. No clients."

Another fragment from Sunday's brunch fell into place. Keith had been dismissive when Andrea said she wanted to return to their party's roots—*"it's too late this year, unfortunately"*—sure she'd change her mind.

"Did your wife have any enemies? Trouble at work? Anyone she was concerned about?"

Other than you, his tone implied. Keith stumbled over what to say. Yes, she'd been concerned about something on Sunday. And he'd ignored her. He rubbed his temples as if the pressure could uncover the truth.

"You never pay attention, Keith. You don't even try to understand."

The uniformed cop who had taken the gun away returned and whispered in the detective's ear. The tension in the room became as brittle as the bourbon-and-Coke coating Keith's mouth earlier. The detective reached for a pair of handcuffs and moved toward him.

"Come with me, Mr. Walton. You're under arrest for the murder of your wife."

Keith swallowed hard against the bile rising in his throat. He knew how it looked. The gun, the booze, the sketchy memories of the party. But he would never hurt his wife. He had to make the detective understand that.

The detective pulled his arms behind him and fastened the cuffs around his wrists.

"What if I told you I'd stumbled across something about one of our clients, something bad?"

"Wait. *Wait.*" Keith pulled back when the detective tried to strong-arm him out of the room. He almost had it. Another broken memory skated just outside his reach. Barry's face twisted in anger, an emotion so uncharacteristic that Keith thought it must be part of a bourbon-fueled nightmare.

"The right thing to do would be to cut our ties with him immediately, before he pulls us down with him."

Two uniformed officers appeared and grabbed Keith's arms, pinning him between them. He twisted, but their grips dug tighter into the flesh of his arms.

"She knew something about him," he thrust his chin toward Barry. "She knew. She tried to tell me but I didn't listen. Oh, god. I didn't listen."

"Don't make this harder than it has to be." The detective actually looked bored.

"Please." Keith locked eyes with his wife's business partner and best friend, the only person in the room who could save him. "She must have talked to you. Tell him."

Tiffany shot him a look of such loathing that he almost missed the relief etched at the corners of her eyes.

"What if I told you I'd stumbled across something about one of our clients, something bad?"

"What does Tiffany say?"

"It's all about money to her."

The detective and the other officers faded into the background until the only people Keith could see were Tiffany and Barry. His wife's best friend. His wife's best client.

"You were in on it together," his voice cracked into a whisper. "You set me up. Which one of you pulled the trigger?"

The memories came faster now. Barry, proud, showing off the fancy bourbon. The three of them toasting to the future.

"Now, wait a minute. You're not going to pin her murder on me." Barry's mild-mannered surfer dude persona disappeared, replaced by desperation and fear.

Tiffany lit another cigarette with shaky fingers. "I'm sorry, Keith. I should have seen he was just using me, setting me up as his alibi."

"You came on to me." Barry looked as sick as Keith felt.

Tiffany's eyes turned to steel. "Andrea knew about your past, Barry. She told me about the embezzlement, but I wanted more proof. I should have believed her."

"Tiffany only cares about the money."

Her story didn't ring true, didn't match his memories, dark and disturbing, that now flashed in rapid-fire succession.

An inept splash of brown liquid in a crystal glass.

A hand wrapped around his, pressing his fingers against cold, gray metal.

The library spinning.

So much blood.

"The right thing to do would be to cut our ties with him immediately, before he pulls us down with him. After the party, I have to end it. I can't live with this on my conscience."

The horrific images, the half-remembered conversation. Keith retched. He knew. He saw the whole thing as if he had been there. Andrea and Tiffany stayed in the yard lighting leftover fireworks long after all the other guests left. Andrea tried to convince Tiffany to drop their star client, to save their business. They argued. Andrea would have insisted on going to the authorities.

"I can't live with this on my conscience."

Tiffany—*she only cares about the money*—saw her life begin to crumble. Desperate to hold on, she left Andrea alone in the yard with her fireworks. She stopped in the library and insisted on one last toast with Keith and Barry, to friendship and the future. Then, she retrieved her best friend's gun from the basement safe and, as the last burst of red-and-blue sparks faded from the night sky, she pulled the trigger.

"Next year will be different, Keith. Just a few friends. No clients. Uncomplicated. I miss the old days, don't you?"

Don't Let the Cop into the House
O'Neil De Noux

The woman with the bag of ice pressed against the side of her face won't look at me. The bald-headed man with the phone pressed against his ear turns to the woman and says, "No answer."

I move out of the way of the SRT commander, our Special Response Team leader Lt. Lenny Schanbein—I went through the academy with Lenny—as he moves through the kitchen to a small den where one of his men holds binoculars to his face and stares out a back window. Schanbein and his men are in all-black, thick flak-vests over their uniform shirts, black helmets on their heads. They look like enraged insects. Beyond the officer with the binocs stands an officer with a sniper rifle.

We're in a small brick house in Lakeview, one that flooded during Katrina and has been pasted back together. The windows where we stand overlook a small back yard with no fence. I see the rear of the house everyone's looking at. There's a sliding glass door that's open. Mike Agrippa sits just inside on a sofa facing the open doorway. He's in an undershirt and has a stainless steel revolver pressed to his right temple.

Sgt. Mike Agrippa is the range officer at the police academy. Never liked me much, but he is efficient, a stickler for safety, which is paramount at a pistol range. Don't know why we've never gotten along, but some cops just don't jell together.

Schanbein seems to notice me for the first time and takes a step my way.

"Detective John Raven Beau." His voice has a snarl to it and his men look at me. "Somebody called Homicide?"

I shake my head. "I was in the neighborhood. Saw all the pretty blue lights outside."

That almost brings a smile.

"Well, let's hope we don't need you."

"How long's he been barricaded?"

"An hour." Schanbein glances at his watch. "Seventy-one minutes exactly."

I nod toward the woman with the ice bag. "His wife?"

"Yep."

"Who's the stiff on the phone?"

"Police psychiatrist." Schanbein gives me a pained look. He's exactly my height, six-two, but heavier. We're both thirty years old.

The stiff hangs up the phone and punches in a number as three more people crowd into the kitchen—a lieutenant, a major and the police chaplain, Father Dennis Leonard moves to the wife and holds her free hand, the one not holding the bag of ice.

I look more closely at her. She's in her forties, her face lined and her hair just starting to gray. They all talk at once and I skirt them toward the back door, which is open. The chaplain shushes them as the wife says, "He never hit me before. Ever." She starts crying, then quickly adds, "He came home angry and I started in on him about the cabinet. Needs fixing." She wipes her eyes and takes in a deep breath. "He blew up. Blows up a lot. Yells but never, never hit me before"—her voice fades and she adds—"now."

I step out the back door and keep going, off the back porch, across the lawn, all the way to Agrippa's house. The back door is open. I step into a kitchen and can see into the den where Agrippa sits on the sofa.

"Sarge?"

He doesn't move so I try again. "Sarge!"

His head turns my way and I nod to him and move through the kitchen. His eyes widen as I ease into the den and immediately sit on a wooden chair that's part of a dining room set that is behind Agrippa. We're about twenty feet apart.

"They sent you?"

"Nobody sent me."

He looks back into the kitchen, then out the open sliding glass door, then back at me. "You're uh. You not supposed to get this close to...someone with a gun to his head."

"I know."

I look around the room. The ceiling's low and the walls are paneled. There's an easy chair and a bigger sofa in front of a big-screen TV on shelves along the far side of the room, which smells of lemon cleaner.

"Why you here?"

I look back at Agrippa. "Came to sit with you."

He readjusts the gun's muzzle against his temple and I see it's a .357 magnum revolver, its hammer already cocked.

"You come to a room with an expert marksman with a gun to his head and just wanna sit? You're crazier than me."

"No one else was coming over," I tell him.

"What if I take you with me?" His voice deepens, anger in it now.

"What would be the point?"

His breathing increases and I feel goose bumps on my arms and can't help staring into his eyes. He moves that gun I gotta jump and pray.

The wildness in his eyes fades and one eye narrows at me.

"OK," he says. "Mister Big Shot Homicide Detective. You talk me outta this and you're a big hero."

I just stare back.

He looks outside again and I pull my gaze from him, looking around the room, realizing I know little about this man. Is he a hunter? Likes to fish? Is he a sports fan? There are no clues in the room. No deer heads on the wall, no stuffed bass or fishing poles. No Saints posters. Just some framed prints—an Audubon pelican, a blue heron, two Dana De Noux tree scenes and black-and-white pictures of St. Louis Cemetery No. 1, ancient crypts and walled tombs.

Agrippa's sweating big time and it's not hot at all. An autumn breeze flows through the house.

"They called Homicide?" he asks.

"Nope."

He looks at me again. "You just the cowboy they *all* wanna be, huh?"

"Cowboy? Unfortunate word for a son of the Sioux."

"Yeah. Sioux. I remember I called you an Injun on the range and you said something about scalping me."

Don't remember that exactly, but I usually warn people who call me *Injun* that it's a racial slur before I show them my Obsidian knife, the one sharpened on one side only, the way the plains warriors sharpen their knives to skin buffalo or take a scalp or two.

The phone rings and we both jump.

"You mind unplugging that damn thing?"

I get up and go over to the phone in the corner and unplug it from the wall. As I sit back down, he goes, "What I don't get is. We never got along. You're a hardhead on the range."

"I'm a hardhead all the time."

Sweat steams down the side of his face. "Why are you really here?"

I look toward the sliding door. "They're all yakking over there, not knowing what the hell to do. I just thought one of us should come over and sit with you until you decide."

"To do it or not, right?"

I nod.

"One of *us*? he snarls. "You gonna start telling me we're all family? Brother cops and all that shit."

I shake my head slowly.

"What's your plan, Mister Detective?"

"Sit here a while."

The man's messed up. His face looks pallid, his eyes are bleary. He's tired, drained. The man's been beaten down. He's gotta be around fifty. Been on the job a good twenty-five, thirty years.

"My wife out there?"

"Yeah."

"How bad did I hurt her?"

"She's got a bag of ice against the side of her face. That's all."

"Get outta here," he snaps at me.

I feel my heart beating now and take in a deep breath.

He looks back out the sliding door.

"I been down a while," he says. "Long time. Tell my wife I love her."

"Tell her yourself."

He turns to me and I see the gun quivering. "You're not gonna talk me outta this. There's nothing you can say or do." He closes his eyes and sucks in a deep breath. "I know all about suicide and temporary depression, but I don't give a rat's ass about that. The pain is real, man." The eyes snap open. "And un…relenting."

"There's medicines…"

"I know!" He glares at me. "I know. Antianxiety pills. Antidepressants. But they won't cure me. Dulling it won't end the pain." He pulls the gun away from his temple and shakes it over his head. "Only *this* will end the pain."

He gasps, takes in another breath and says, "I hit my wife, man. I *hit* her."

He shoves the muzzle against his temple and I hear my heart stammering in my ears as the seconds tick by, slow and purposeful.

"I brought the anger. I took it out on her." His eyes are moist now. "I let the cop into the house. I *brought* him in." A tear starts down the man's face. "I brought all the shit we do out there, all of it, into the house and took it out on her."

81

He leans back on the sofa and closes his eyes again, the gun shaking now.

"I been bringing the cop home for years. Yelling. Breaking things. *But I never hit her.* Ever."

My cell phone rings and I almost jump out of the chair. I turn it off without looking at it, and Agrippa's staring at me again. His eyes are asking if I know what he means. And I hope my eyes tell him yeah, I do.

We both know the monster that dwells in us, how we use it in verbal confrontations with people—the cursing, the screaming at people to let it out so you don't pummel some smart-ass to death. We see too much shit, and most of the time we're unable to do anything except slap handcuffs on wrists. When we came out of the academy, it was us against the bad guys. It didn't take long for it to be us against everyone who didn't wear blue. Everyone...even our kin.

"Must be easy for you," Agrippa says. "How many you shot?"

No. He thinks that since I was able to do what so many cops dream of doing, of personally ending a criminal career, I've found relief. But there's no relief.

"How many?"

"Five."

"Remind me," he says, and that's good. If he wants me to talk about it, if he wants to hear about it, maybe, just maybe we can pass some time, maybe this will...deflate.

"The first was outside the Second District Station," I begin. "Man in a cowboy outfit."

"Yeah," Agrippa says, "I heard about it."

"Man in a ten-gallon hat, leather vest, boots and spurs, two nickel-plated revolvers in a double holster rig."

"He shot at some cops, right?"

"Went up and dared three cops to *draw.* They laughed, so he pulled out both six guns and peppered the front of the stationhouse.

I dropped him with two shots. Caught hell for it. Indian kills cowboy."

He nods, eyes closed again. "What about number two?"

"Armed robber from the K&B, Carrollton and Claiborne, got into a running gun battle with ten units. Fifty-four shots fired by police. Three hit the robber. All mine. The next was a rape-in-progress call. Rapist charged at me with a butcher knife. Then I shot the man who shot Cassandra Smith.

"Cop killer."

"Got him in Exchange Alley."

"That's four."

"The last one was in Bayou Sauvage."

"Don't know that one."

"Another cop killer. Clyde Pailet."

Clyde was a swamp rat and drew me into the swamp, only I'm half Cajun and was raised on Vermilion Bay. Half Sioux and half Cajun. Deadly combination that Pailet discovered.

I don't go into the shootings right after Katrina. That wasn't me, anyway. It was some sort of shadow-warrior, hunting down vermin. And as I sit here, I wonder if that's what's kept me from putting a gun against the side of my head. Has killing let me release the pressure, let the steam out?

"I never shot anyone," he says.

"Then you're lucky."

Sgt. Mike Agrippa opens his eyes and smiles at me and the hair stands out on my arms. No. *Don't smile*. Don't—

The explosion is loud in the confines of the room. It reverberates as his blood and brains fly through the air. His body quivers and slowly slides to the floor. I realize I'm surprised he actually did it. I didn't think he'd go through with it. I go over and see the top of his head is gone and know it's no use.

Footsteps rush in behind me. Schanbein and two E.M.T.s push by, one carrying a medical bag. I back away and go out the sliding door. The man with the binoculars is staring at me, and I turn my face to the distant sun and close my eyes.

The widow stands in the back door of the house as I cross the yard. She watches me through tear-filled eyes. I walk up and look down into them and she slowly shakes her head.

"What happened?" asks the major.

"Ask the guy with the binocs," I say as I keep looking to the widow's eyes.

"What the hell were you thinking?" This from the lieutenant.

"I want a full report," stammers the major. "Report for debriefing."

"I'll put it in a daily."

"No daily report. I want a full report. You're gonna be debriefed by the police psychiatrist."

A familiar face appears next to me and my lieutenant steps between the major and me.

"This is a Homicide Case," says Lt. Dennis Merten. "I'm in charge now, and he'll put it in a daily."

The widow's hand grabs mine as I start to move away.

"Did he say anything?"

"He was sorry he hit you. He said he loved you."

She's a strong woman, standing there staring at me, wiping the tears from her face.

"They told me who you are. You're not one of Mike's friends. Why'd you go over there?"

"Nobody else was going."

For now that's it. Later, I'll drop in on her and tell her about the cop we shouldn't let into the house. I'll tell her later.

Rosie's Choice
John M. Floyd

Rosie Cartwright was sipping coffee and knitting a blue sweater for her grandson when she heard the tinkle of the bell on the front door of the shop. The two men who pushed through the door and into the air-conditioning weren't typical customers. Both were stiff and solemn, and looked uncomfortable in their dark blue blazers. (It was, after all, early July.) Mostly, though, they were unusual because they weren't women. Notions Eleven attracted mostly female shoppers.

Once inside, the men seemed to avoid her gaze, pausing instead to examine the shelves and islands of knickknacks—at least that's what Rosie called them—between the door and the counter where she sat. Rosie, who had put aside little Martin's sweater and had already opened her mouth to say, "Can I help you," shut it again and resumed her knitting. "Let browsers browse," her daughter Nancy had instructed her.

Rosie could hear the POP-POP-POP of fireworks somewhere outside and down the street. Irritating but understandable—tomorrow was Independence Day. There were always a few people who liked to start celebrating early.

She took another swallow of coffee.

After a minute or so the older and shorter of the two men looked up and caught her eye. "Notions Eleven," he said, nodding toward the big backward letters on the shop's front window. "What's it mean?"

Good question, Rosie thought. The store's contents included everything from upscale glassware to tacky household ornaments—but they weren't really "notions." According to her dictionary, notions were items used in sewing—needles, buttons, pins, that kind of thing. Nancy had just liked the name. She had also liked that movie, *Ocean's Eleven*. "You'd have to ask my daughter," Rosie said. "It's her shop."

The short man frowned. He and his partner exchanged a glance. "You're not Nancy Bartlett?"

"I'm Rosie Cartwright—her mother. If you came to see Nancy, she just left for lunch."

He nodded thoughtfully. "And left you, as they say, minding the store."

"Tough duty," Rosie said, holding up her knitting. "I suppose I'll get used to it."

The short man had picked up a tiny porcelain elephant and was examining it. "Used to it?"

"I'm new here. Just moved to town last week, from the East Coast." Then, without really meaning to, she added, "I recently lost my husband."

"Sorry to hear it."

But his eyes, Rosie thought, didn't look sorry at all. They didn't look as if he cared one way or the other.

Outside, the distant fireworks popped and banged.

She glanced down at the gold watch on her wrist—the only thing she owned of any real value. Twelve twenty-eight. Nancy would be gone until one fifteen or so. "The truth is," Rosie said, "my daughter doesn't really need full-time help. Since you know her name, you probably know she's only been open a month. But I'm part owner, and now that I live here, and I'm alone...well, I suppose I needed something to do."

"Then maybe you need us as well. You and Nancy both."

"What do you mean?"

Instead of replying, the short man said one word, over his shoulder, "Charles?"

Behind him, the other man nodded, walked the ten paces to the front door, and twisted the old-fashioned toggle that locked the door from the inside. The metallic sound was loud in the quiet room. Then he reversed the cardboard sign hanging in the window.

Anyone approaching the door from the sidewalk would now see the word CLOSED.

Her heart pounding, Rosie watched him return. When she looked again at the shorter man—the boss?—his face was blank, his expression neither happy nor sad, angry nor friendly. For a moment they studied each other in silence. A clock somewhere in the shop struck the half-hour.

Finally he said, "What I mean is, we offer protection."

"Protection from what?"

"From anything. Robbery, burglary, assault, vandalism, you name it. It's not a bad area, Ms. Cartwright, but—as you might've noticed—this isn't Beverly Hills. You never know who might walk in, or what they might do."

"What they might do?"

"To you," he said, "or to your property." As he spoke the last word of the sentence, he opened his hand. The little porcelain elephant fell to the hardwood floor and shattered into a hundred glittering pieces.

Neither of them looked down at the damage. Their eyes remain locked. With a great effort, Rosie kept her face impassive, her voice steady. "And you," she said, "will protect me from these things?"

"Just as we protect the other businesses in your neighborhood." He moved closer, crunching through the broken porcelain until he faced her from the other side of the counter. "All of them have agreements with us. Isn't that right, Charles?"

"That's right, Mr. Davis." The taller man was leaning against a bank of shelves ten feet away, one hand in his pocket and the other resting beside a row of crystal vases. As Rosie watched, one of his fat fingers nudged the largest of the vases an inch closer to the edge of its shelf.

She focused on Davis. "You two aren't from around here either, are you?"

"You recognized our accents?" He stroked his chin as if deciding whether he needed a shave. "You're right, of course—

we're transplants too. Charles and I conducted this same sort of service in New York until our relocation some time ago. Years of experience in the industry, one might say."

"Until they ran you out of town?"

For the first time, Davis smiled. "Until we recognized the greater rewards of sunny California. The only disadvantage is access—visiting our clients here involves a car. In the Apple we could walk everywhere, or catch the occasional taxi." He studied her a moment. "Your accent is familiar as well. Manhattan?"

"For a while. And Brooklyn."

"Small world. What did you do, there?"

"We worked together, my husband and I."

"Of course." He glanced over her shoulder, at a wall clock that had the twelve astrological signs instead of numbers. "I can't say I'm not enjoying our chat, Ms. Cartwright, but I don't have all day. I assume you'll agree to do business with us?"

Rosie cleared her throat. "What would that involve, exactly?"

"It would involve the payment of a thousand dollars a month," he said. "To Charles here."

She could feel the beginnings of hot tears in her eyes, but made herself blink them away. A protection racket, of all things. Extortion. Part of her couldn't believe it was really happening.

Oh, Tom, she thought. *I wish you were here with me.*

"Do I have a choice?" she asked.

"Charles, what do you think? Does she have a choice?"

The tall man responded by moving his finger slightly, and the vase tipped off the edge of the shelf. This time Rosie looked at it, watched it fall. Watched it break. What would Nancy think, Rosie wondered, if she came back at this moment, found the door locked and the CLOSED sign up, looked through the glass, and saw what was happening? What would she *do*? Bang on the door? Unlock it and barge in? Faint? Nancy was the kind of person who wigged out if she saw a spider, or got a paper cut. Rosie thanked God she wasn't here.

"The first payment," Davis informed her, "is due today."

She looked up at him. "Today?"

"In cash, if you don't mind."

Rosie swallowed, breathing hard. "Does anyone ever refuse?"

Davis frowned as if trying to recall. "Three people, so far." He held up fingers and ticked each of them off: "Old man Renfroe, down the street, wound up with a broken leg. Told everyone he fell down the stairs in his apartment. The Chinese gentleman who owns the cleaners half a mile east must've left the gas on one night—his place blew up and burned to the ground. And the pop in the mom-and-pop grocery three doors down stepped in front of a car on the way home from their store late one afternoon. A sad thing, that. He was only fifty or so. His wife is now a client."

Rosie felt her stomach roiling, felt cold sweat break out on her forehead. *Stay calm,* she thought. Somewhere to the south, a whole string of firecrackers went off at once, making her jump. They sounded like the rattle of a machine gun.

"What about the police?" she said. "Weren't they suspicious?"

"Why should they be? They were accidents. No accusations were made. No accusations will ever be made. Even if someone does, and is brave or foolish enough to testify, nothing'll come of it. I run a legitimate business a mile away. Davis Building Supply. Besides"—Davis shrugged—"I have connections."

"With the cops, you mean?"

"With whomever I need to keep operating. Call them 'silent partners.'"

She paused, trying to think. "Who's your boss? I'd like to speak to him."

Davis moved a step closer. "I'm the boss, Ms. Cartwright. I answer to no one. Charles here is my only employee. He handles payments."

"Does Charles handle what happens when payments aren't made?"

Another smile. "We subcontract for that kind of work. But when we have to"—he pulled back one side of his blazer to reveal a shoulder holster—"we can do that ourselves, too."

Without being told, the taller man leaned a bit farther back, exposing the grip of a pistol tucked into his waistband.

"A day like today, for example," Davis said, nodding toward the door and the occasional sounds of celebration. "Nobody'd pay any attention to a gunshot or two."

A long silence passed. Rosie stared at Davis and the two men stared at Rosie. Outside, the rest of the world went on its merry way, unknowing and uncaring about the drama playing out inside Notions Eleven. From the corner of her eye she saw a middle-aged woman pause in front of the door, apparently read the sign, and continue down the sidewalk.

"I don't have a thousand dollars," Rosie said.

Davis's smile faded. "Look and see."

"Look where? You think Nancy keeps that kind of money in the cash register?"

"I think she keeps it in a safe. That's what most businesses around here do."

"We don't have a safe."

"Yes you do." Davis's gaze flicked down to the countertop and back again. "Until recently this was a flower shop, and the guy who owned it had a vault underneath the counter, right where you're sitting. It was built-in and anchored, so it's still there."

"Why are you so sure we would use it?"

"Why would you not use it?" he asked.

A sudden but logical question occurred to her. "How do you know all this?" Rosie asked. "How *could* you know it?"

"Because the florist shop was one of our customers."

"That's impossible. Nancy said she knew the owner. He would've told her about you, before selling the place to her."

Davis shook his head. "No. He wouldn't have."

Rosie realized that was the truth. Men like these would be a threat not only to those who lived and worked here, but also to those who had moved on. They wouldn't forget. And Nancy wasn't the most savvy businesswoman in the world anyway. In fact she was a bit of a scatterbrain, and even more so since her divorce. Why else had Rosie and Tom Cartwright offered to help her with almost half the money to buy the shop?

"Go ahead, Ms. Cartwright. Check the safe. Make the payment. Or would you rather we wait until your daughter gets back from lunch?" Davis tilted his head and regarded her a moment. "We can do that, you know. I would so enjoy meeting her."

Rosie felt her mouth go dry. Her mind was spinning.

He was right. *Do whatever it takes, whatever you have to do*, she told herself—*but don't allow Nancy to be a part of all this.*

With a deep sigh Rosie stooped forward from her seat, reached below the counter, spun the combination of the vault, and opened its steel door. She could hear herself breathing, could feel her hand trembling. Still bent over, she looked up at Davis.

"Let me get this straight," she said. "If I don't pay you, here and now...you'll kill me?"

He looked shocked. "Certainly not."

"You won't?"

"Of course not. You said you were part owner." Davis leaned toward her, smiled, and said, softly but distinctly, "We'll kill your daughter."

She looked at Charles and saw that he was grinning also. Secretly, she was glad they were. It helped her make up her mind.

Rosie sat up and raised her hand above the counter—but it wasn't holding a thousand dollars. It was holding the gun she'd stored on the shelf beside the safe, her late husband's .38 revolver.

She shot Davis once, in the middle of the forehead, and even before he hit the floor she shifted left and shot Charles too. He was farther away but he was bigger so she aimed for the center of his chest and fired three times.

She sat there for several seconds, ears ringing, then calmly set her gun down beside her knitting, removed a handkerchief from her purse, and walked around the counter. Both men were stone dead, lying on their backs with arms flung wide, as if terminally tired of shopping. A pungent, smoky smell lingered in the air. Careful not to kneel in the spreading pools of blood, she used her handkerchief to remove Davis's pistol and place it in his outstretched hand. She did the same thing with Charles's gun, a big black automatic.

Then Rosie tiptoed her way back to the counter and called 9-1-1. She directed the police to come to the rear alley entrance—she didn't want to disturb the fingerprints Charles would have left on the front door's lock and the OPEN/CLOSED sign—and then called Nancy's cell phone to tell her the same thing. When that was done she hung up, tucked the handkerchief back into her purse, marched to the back of the shop to unlock the alley door, and returned to the counter to sit down on her stool and wait for the cavalry.

She felt more at ease than she thought she would be. Her heartbeat was back to an almost-normal rate, and her hands weren't shaking quite so badly. Would the police believe her story? She didn't know. But she felt she'd have plenty of support from the neighboring businesses that had been fleeced over the years. And she knew what her husband Tom would have said: *You did the right thing, Rosie.*

She took a slow sip from her coffee cup—the one with the words WORLD'S BEST GRANDMA written on the side—and checked the time again on her gold wristwatch.

The one with the words ROSE CARTWRIGHT, 25 YEARS, NYPD engraved on the back.

Don't Be Cruel

JoAnne Lucas

Fresno, California
Tuesday, June 5, 1957

Homicide Detective Frank Ransom slowed his Ford at the restaurant's driveway. He played with the idea that the scene ahead was a wide-angle camera shot of the parking lot. It took in the rose and aqua neon on the roof of the diner down to two black-and-white cruisers adding more color with their revolving cherries, and panned over to a gray sedan like his parked nearby in the background. Boy, howdy, put it all in glorious Technicolor, maybe with Vista Vision and zoom in for a close-up of the opened front door. Enter the story through its portal. Even has Stereophonic Sound, he mused, as the same kind of bebop music his kids liked bullied its way outside. *Hold, and cut. Great production shot. Needed a few dragsters parked nearby, maybe James Dean slouching against the wall. Damned shame what happened to him. Three films and he's gone.*

Ransom doused his imaginary movie and finished driving into the lot, parking on the far side of a patrol car and the unmarked police sedan. He donned his seersucker jacket and summer fedora, and picked up a notebook and sketch pad as he nodded at the man getting out of the other sedan. Unusual for Greely to beat him to the call. He noted that the young detective just missed leading man's status. Had the height and breadth like Victor Mature, but also a bad haircut, narrow mouth, wrong nose for the face, and ears that stuck out. No, Detective David Greely could never be a heartthrob in Hollywood. Good thing he decided to be one of Fresno's finest instead.

A light wind played Red Rover with papers Frank had left on his dash, and he lunged to grab them as they fluttered their way out of his window and across Greely's car hood. "Ha! Got you, you little rascals. Breeze sure feels good after the scorcher we had today, doesn't it?"

93

Greely agreed. "I heard the call and was a few blocks over. Came by to see if you could use some help—maybe direct the uniforms out here."

"'Preciate it. Downtown's short-handed tonight, so we're in for a wait. Send in the doc and photo and prints right away, but make the morgue's boys cool their heels." He saw the wind was blowing the younger man's hair. *Humph, needs a haircut.*

Litter scurried for attention across the asphalt and the neon zizzed. The patrol car's motor pinged and he felt the heat radiating off its hood. Ransom took a deep breath. *This is where it all stops being a movie scenario.* In spite of his resolve, a voice in his head shouted, *roll 'em!* as he continued through the open doorway.

The strong scent of a thousand fries and burgers served over the years taunted his nose and sent an urgent call to his stomach, unhappy that he'd skipped dinner. He pacified it by popping a peppermint Lifesaver in his mouth and continued to survey the area. No one in the diner but the grill cook with a mug of coffee and a police officer leaning against the soda counter. Ransom observed the juke was just starting to play H-16 as he passed. He could see the victim's legs from the foyer and quickly moved around the register counter to view the corpse on the floor.

Well, hello, Marilyn Monroe! He leaned closer. *No—not a Marilyn, bigger girl, more like a Jayne Mansfield. Must be 5'8". Bet she was trouble. Bet she liked playing with fire. Finally got some guy too angry. Manually strangled. Passionate, intimate kind of death, don't see many of them, thank God. Hard way to die. What did she do to drive a man to such a deed?* He cast an eye over her tight-fitting waitress uniform with its pink and white checked waist apron, down to her feet. *Huh! Nylons and white flats. No big ugly, comfortable bucks and bobby sox for our Jayne. Figures.*

Ransom regarded a splay of quarters on the floor, most had red enamel disfiguring them. It looked like they had been in the small pottery bowl that lay shattered nearby. He pulled out his book and quickly sketched the crime scene, the short hallway beyond, and the rest of the diner. Black-and-white photos would come his way later. Right now he could do without the constant flashes and chatter of the cameraman and expended bulbs littering the place. He noted time, distances, and colors on each drawing.

Somewhere he realized the song had finished and a new record was due to play. *Thank Hannah, that last one seemed to go on forever.* But, no—this sounded like the same one. He eyed the lighted tabs on the machine. Huh! H-16 again.

"That's ole Elvis the Pelvis."

Ransom looked over at the speaker. *Grill cook, white tee shirt, dungarees, food-splattered apron. Late forties, maybe fifty, skinny, 5'5", pasty complexion.* "You the one phoned in the murder?"

"Yeah. Name's Louis Kelly." He coughed the hard smokers' hack.

"See who did it, Louis?"

"Call me Kelly. Nah, took a break in the alley. When I came back in that song was playin' and nobody was here."

"Same song?"

He nodded. "It's 'Don't Be Cruel.' Tell ya the truth, I like Elvis, but I'm gettin' sick of that song."

"So, this same song's been playing, what eight, ten times?"

"I guess."

"Think it's stuck?"

"Shouldn't be, juke got serviced today."

Ransom beckoned to the cop. "Officer—?"

"Collins, sir."

"Collins, good. Try and remember how many times you've heard this song since you've been here and the next time it starts over, time it. Also time what it takes to end and start again. Then call dispatch and get when the call came in. See if the dispatcher remembers hearing the music. Figure when the dispatcher called you and when you arrived. Don't let doc or the evidence guys touch that jukebox unless I'm here." He just might get lucky and pinpoint a close time of the murder. Now if he could make Kelly open up more.

"Ah, Kelly—"

"You mind if we go out back? I'm not allowed to smoke in the kitchen. Health rules. And it don't feel right smokin' here with Barbara dead 'n all."

"Sure, we'll go out back."

They walked through the kitchen, past the huge refrigerator and stocked shelves, and out the screen door.

"Grab a crate and set yourself down," Kelly said. "Smoke?"

"No thanks."

Kelly lit a Lucky while Ransom sketched the alley. He drew the wooden crates and cardboard boxes neatly stacked against the building, the refuse overflowing three dented galvanized cans, the number of fresh butts littering the ground around Kelly's overturned crate.

"So, Kelly, you Navy?" He indicated the cook's forearm tattoos.

"Yeah, did the duty for Uncle Sam during the war." Kelly stretched his arms forward for Ransom to see better. "Learned to cook on the *Missouri*."

"Proud ship."

The cook smiled.

"Looks like you had yourself a smoke fest here tonight."

Kelly scuffed at the butts. "Guess I did at that." He looked a little sheepish. "I clean 'em up after my last break of the night."

"You smoke this much all the time?"

"Well, it being Tuesday and all, not much business. I'd finished my orders, so I turned off the grill and came out for some solitude— jus' listenin' to the stories of the night."

Ransom wished he hadn't turned down that cigarette, and reached for another Lifesaver. "Uh-huh. What kind of stories do you hear?"

"Well, sir, I can tell the difference between an ambulance and a fire truck and a cop car pretty much by how fast they's travelin'. And I can hear when a car comes and leaves here. Make a bet with myself 'bout what make it is and who's inside."

"That right?"

"Yeah. Teenagers always come in with their music blaring, wanting to share. If it's a family, I listen to how many doors open and shut. And a loner will always order quicker than the others. Helps me figure how soon I need to get back inside and fire up the grill. Gets hot in there with it goin' all the time, y'know?"

Ransom allowed how that would be the case. "What happened tonight?"

"I cooked up my last burger for a regular—no mayo, double pickles and fries—'bout eight ten. Barbara was in a mood, fairly slapped the order on his table and sat back behind the register to file her nails. Figured this a good time for a smoke. She's a mean one when she gets goin'. Almost finished my first butt when I heard that hard case on a motorcycle drive in. A real punk, that one. Thinks he's the Marlon Brando of Fresno. Calls hisself Duke. Always lookin' for a free burger, and I din't feel like obligin' him tonight. Often him and Barbara would have them a heavy make-out session in that little hallway. I thought screw it, and had me 'nother ciggie. Heard the biker leave. He really laid down some rubber."

"You think he killed her and got scared?"

"Nah, he's got girls all over town. If anyone was mad, it was Barbara. Her shift din't end 'til ten and she couldn't go with him. No more cars came, none left. Heard some dishes break and figured I really din't need to be involved in that mess. By then I was thinkin' 'bout doing a third smoke when Elvis came on. That 'Don't Be Cruel' song. So I leaned back and enjoyed myself." He coughed hard, hawked, and spat. "Nasty habit. Someday I'll quit."

"Yeah, me too."

"Speaking of Brando, you see him in *Teahouse of the August Moon* yet? Had to keep remindin' myself it was really him. Never seen him in such a part before."

"Know what you mean. Sure wasn't *On the Waterfront* or *Streetcar*. I think he just enjoyed doing the role and it spilled out all over the audience."

"Yeah, that's it exactly." They sat in companionable silence, Ransom busy with a new drawing and Kelly lost in his thoughts.

"Y'know," Kelly squinted against the curling smoke, "I 'member you. Used to come in Rose's on Belmont four, five years ago. Chicken-fried steak well, side of horseradish, extra catsup."

"Huh, well I'll be. How'd you do that?"

"I always remember regulars."

"Well, I haven't had a good chicken-fried steak since you left. Isn't that something." Ransom added some more shading to his sketch. "Say, Kelly, what's the best movie you've seen in the last two years?"

"*Mr. Roberts*, hands down. Saw it four times at the Tower. Y'know, you remind me of Henry Fonda in that movie—all lean, soft-spoken, but strong on duty."

"Well, thanks." He chuckled. "Never been thought of as a movie star before. 'Preciate it."

Kelly cackled.

Definitely a Walter Brennan with tattoos.

Ransom let Kelly smoke in silence then said, "You get six picks for a quarter on the jukebox. If somebody were to put several quarters in and hit H-16 for each selection, you'd get pretty much what we're getting now. That right? "

Kelly agreed.

"I gotta ask you, what's with those quarters on the floor being red?" "Them's the ones we salt the juke with to get the customers in the mood. We paint 'em with nail polish. When Ernie comes every week to work on the juke, he pulls out all the reds and returns 'em to us. Then he divvies the rest, gives half to the diner and keeps the other half."

"And Ernie was here today?"

"Yep, late. 'Bout four thirty. Truck broke down."

"Had many people played it since then?

"Nope, it being Tuesday and all. Friday'd be a different story."

"What do you think happened here?" Ransom asked.

"Dunno. Maybe some bum come in off the street. Nah, no bum would've left all them quarters there—or the register take."

Ransom agreed.

"Maybe an old boyfriend. Parked on the street and sneaked in the exit. No, I'da still heard the car, 'less he parked maybe a half block away or more."

Kelly looks worried, Ransom thought. Should be. If I believe him, and damned if I don't, then no one could have come into the diner and killed Barbara. "You sure you didn't hear another car come or leave?"

"No sir. Wisht I had. Couldn't have missed something like that. I listen all the time. There's just no way. It's important to my job."

As if on cue, both men became alert with the sound of a couple of cars pulling into the front lot. Each car only opened one door. Ransom sighed and closed his sketchbook. "Might be the doc. We'd better go in."

Frank let the swinging service door bump his back as he stopped suddenly. *Something's different.* "Officer Collins," he called.

"Right here," said Collins, exiting the men's room in the hall. "Detective Greely said he'd keep everyone out 'til I was done," he indicated the bathroom. "Got that information you wanted and figured out a timetable for you."

Ransom nodded and pulled out his sketchbook. A quick comparison showed that a hat from a booth coat rack was missing. He called to Kelly to follow him over to the booth. "You remember this order?" he gestured to the plate.

"Sure do. My last one, Mr. No Mayo and Double Pickles. Looks like he wasn't hungry."

"He a regular for sure?"

"Every night, same thing. Don't come for my cookin'. Got a crush on Barbara. My God she was a witch. I'd watch her play guys like this for suckers, always getting little presents from them for a smile. No present, she'd turn on the frost. Even got one guy to spring for a fancy vacuum with all sorts of attachments. Poor slobs. She just toyed with 'em for kicks." He shook his head. "Gave women a bad name."

"What'd he look like?"

"Just a suit, like you. Always dressed like he was going to church or court. Big guy."

"He have a hat?"

"Said he was a suit, 'course he had a hat."

"Right, right."

Ransom sat directly behind Mr. Double Pickles' booth and looked around. This would pretty much be Pickles' line of sight. He noticed he had a good view of the short hallway leading to the restrooms, and didn't like what he was thinking of next. Of how the patrol car's engine was still hot enough to ping and give off heat, but that Greely's car hood had been cool when he caught his papers on it. And that Kelly swore no cars had left the lot after he went outside for his smoke. He thought about how someone wearing a suit would have had his arms protected from Barbara's nails in her struggles and how it would take a tall, husky man to throttle her, a man who had been cruelly played. "Don't Be Cruel," indeed. Then he remembered the wind in Greely's hair and how a fedora had gone missing while Collins was taking a leak. He pulled in a deep, sharp breath and sent Kelly to the kitchen and Collins outside to summon the young detective.

Greely stuck his head in the doorway. "Sir, I think I'd better stay out here. More press just drove up."

"Oh, I think the men can handle it. Come on in, I need you here. Take a look at the record that's playing, but don't touch the juke box. Now, doesn't it look a little warped and that's why it keeps playing over and over?" Greely did as he was told. "Can't really tell, but yeah, I think it's warped."

"You don't think it's because someone fed maybe three, four quarters to the machine and rigged that song? Someone who'd got a rude awakening tonight when his dream girl made out with a street punk practically in front of him? Most men couldn't take that without going crazy. I figure we'll be able to lift his prints from H-16 and those red quarters when we get Ernie back here to open the money box. No—don't move. Officer Collins, cuffs please. Kelly, come on out. This your Mr. No Mayo, Double Pickles?" Greely tried to jerk away, but Collins had got the cuffs on. Kelly identified him positively.

Tears flowed down Greely's face. It wasn't pretty. *No, Greely was no leading man like Gregory Peck, but he wasn't a villain either. The man's whole body grieved. More like that great character actor, Victor McLaglan, who grabbed your heart and made you weep with him. It was just a damned shame.* "Take it easy, son," Ransom said. "Tell us about it. It'll go easier on you."

*

Hours later with the police work done, the diner's owner came to lock up. Out front in the parking lot Ransom gave Kelly the sketch he did of him in the alley.

"You do this while we was talkin'?"

"Yep. Hobby of mine."

"It's a damned good one. Would you, y'know, sign it or somthin'?"

"I'd be pleased to." He wrote an inscription to Louis Kelly and signed the picture.

"Say, Frank, this is really nice of you. Tell you what. Come on down anytime, I'll fix you a chicken-fried well with horseradish on the side and extra catsup. Bring the wife and kids."

"Done. I'll look forward to it." He shook hands with the cook and couldn't help saying in his best Bogie voice, "'Louie, this looks like the beginning of a beautiful friendship.'"

"Ha! *Casablanca*. Best dammed movie ever made. See ya around, cop."

Detective Frank Ransom walked across the lot to his car just as the diner's lights turned off, leaving only the noisy neon to guard against the night.

Fade to black and cut.

A Simple Job
Andrew MacRae

Years ago, the guy who taught me the tricks of the detective trade had a sign over his desk. "There's No Such Thing as a Simple Job." He'd point to it, usually when I explained how simple a new job was going to be.

My new client said her name was Brigid Morgan. She looked like a Brigid Morgan. She had a freckled face and red hair tied back in a bouncy ponytail, and I was as certain as any stranger could be that the color was natural. Her outfit was an attempt at schoolmarm strict, but the starched white blouse and long skirt failed to keep secret her curves.

Green eyes flashed from behind wire-framed glasses. "Do I meet your approval?"

Busted.

"Sorry, occupational hazard. We're trained to observe and sometimes…"

"Sometimes you get distracted?" A playful smile flirted on her lips.

She had a sense of humor, nice in a client.

Her story was straight, simple and familiar. Someone was blackmailing her, and she wasn't coy giving the details. "Fifteen years ago I allowed myself to be photographed. I was eighteen, broke, and newly arrived in the city." Though her voice was cool and calm, her fingers never stopped twining. "I had honestly managed to forget about it, until…" She fumbled in her purse and brought out a small cardboard envelope, and passed it to me.

I squeezed the sides and let a folded sheet of paper slip from inside, then used a pen and straightened paperclip to unfold and hold the paper open. There were a few lines of text and a color image, a scan of an old-school 35mm print. While decidedly pornographic, the lighting and framing demonstrated that the photographer had considerable skill. Nor was there doubt that it was indeed my client in the photo, or that her hair was naturally red.

I let the lower half of the paper fold back over the picture, leaving only the message. It was short and not very sweet:

This photo and others will be mailed to your board of directors unless you meet my demands.

They wanted twenty-five thousand dollars every three months, delivered in eCoins, a new online banking system used by computer gamers, and fast becoming a preferred method to launder money. There wouldn't be much chance of tracking the payments once they entered the eCoin servers.

Twenty-five grand was a lot of money, but I guessed anyone with a board of directors wasn't worried on that score. Her name rang a bell. "Aren't you the new CEO of Goober, the search engine?"

Ms. Morgan nodded, but kept her lips tight. My client was a fast-rising, young star of high-tech. By all reports, as technically savvy as she was good looking, she was fast shaking up the nerd boy world.

"Let's cut to the chase. What do you want me to do?"

"I want you to find the person blackmailing me."

"That shouldn't be too difficult. Ten to one it's the original photographer, or someone who has his files. The real question is, if and when I find him, what happens next?"

"Simple. I turn him over to the authorities." The lady was cool.

"Won't that cause the very thing you want to avoid? Those pictures may not leak to the press, but the news of them will."

"That will happen no matter what I do. That's something I've already accepted. Instead of asking the police for help, I will turn the bastard over to the D.A. for prosecution. The board might squirm, but the newspapers will love it. I'll be the woman victim who fought back."

Did I mention she was cool?

I brought out my notebook. "Let's get down what you know. Do you remember the photographer's name, or the name of his studio?"

"His name was Rich, if that's any help. He was tall, thin, maybe in his forties, wore wireframe glasses. He seemed professional. I mean, he didn't try to do anything, you know?"

I knew.

"Do you remember where the shoot took place? The date?"

The next quarter-hour was spent with me asking questions and receiving little in return.

"I told you, I buried every memory of it. I don't want to remember." Brigid's voice was close to breaking and her brilliant green eyes awash with tears. A humming noise came from her purse and she brought out a cell phone. "I have to go." She tried, but couldn't keep relief out of her voice.

I figured I had enough to start, so after she gave me a check, I let her go do whatever the CEO of a large corporation does these days.

*

Knowledge of the city is important in my business. I recognized the brand printed on the mailer and knew it was sold exclusively at FedUps stores, having sent a few myself. I also knew the postal code on the envelope and knew there was a FedUps store close to that post office. I took the N-Tamar tram down to Sunset and then hiked three blocks to the corner of Nineteenth and Carlson where a sleek FedUps store pitched its glare at a scruffy little post office across the street.

I went inside and waited until the sales clerk finished a sale and his customer left. It was time to let him know I was no customer.

"Good afternoon. What can I do for you?" Paul, according to his nametag, was somewhere in the neighborhood of forty, paunchy, pale skin, red face, wisps of thin blond hair carefully arranged, a clip-on tie askew.

I let his question hang in the air until concern started to slip into his eyes, and then showed him the mailer, obscuring my client's name and address. I pointed to a rack of others identical to it on the counter and pitched my voice lower, with what I hoped was a tone of authority tinged with a touch of menace. "I want you to think carefully, Paul. Two days ago someone came in and bought one of these."

"Mister, we sell lots of those every day. How can you expect me to remember selling one?"

I ignored what he said and kept speaking in the same, insistent tone. "This person bought the mailer, walked over to that counter, and wrote an address on it. He put a sheet of paper into it." I removed a paper from my jacket, folded it, and stuffed it in the envelope and mimed sealing it.

Paul nodded. "Yeah, yeah, I remember."

"And after he left, you watched him cross the street to mail it at the post office, instead of here."

His eyes widened. "I don't know how you did that, Mister. But you got it right. Well, except..."

"Except?"

"He bought the last one. I remember because I had to refill the display afterwards." Paul described the man. Early to mid-sixties, he was tall, thin, wore wireframe glasses, kind of worn looking, if I knew what he meant. I did.

"Pay by card?"

"Yes." He cast a furtive look around. "I guess it wouldn't hurt to look him up." He punched some keys on the computer and scrolled through a listing. "See, here it is." He pronounced the customer's name slowly as though tasting it for sin. "Rich Rosenthal. What'd he do? Something bad?"

"That's right." I leaned over the counter and checked the display. The address was in a sketchy neighborhood not too far away.

I headed for the door, but before I left I turned back. "And I'm going to catch him, thanks to you."

I left him with a look of accomplishment on his chubby face.

*

I sent Ms. Morgan a text message before leaving the parking lot, letting her know I had found Rich Rosenthal and had his address.

Her reply came fast. "OMG fast!!! Txt 2me pls TY."

Kids these days. I sent her the info, and that was the end of a simple job. As a reward, I took myself to a showing of *Gun Crazy* at the Castro. Peggy Cummins. Now there was a woman who knew how to wear a sweater.

An hour later, with whispered apologies and stepping on toes, I left the theater. I had ignored her first attempts to text and call me, but she was a client who would not be ignored.

"Yes, Ms. Morgan?" I had to raise my voice. The Castro district at night was washed with neon, perfumed with uncollected garbage, and noisy with people out for a good time.

"I want you to go with me." This was a summons, not a request.

"To the police?"

"Yes. Where are you? I'll pick you up."

She misinterpreted my slow consideration for hesitation. "I'll pay you a thousand dollars."

That cured any hesitation on my part. For a quick grand I could neglect pretty Peggy. Besides, *Gun Crazy* was playing all week. I told Ms. Morgan where she could find me, and leaned against a streetlight at the corner of Sixteenth and Mission to wait. In retrospect, not a good idea, as I received a constant stream of offers of service from women, and more than a few men.

A classic, powder-blue 1972 Triumph TR6, in not-so-classic condition, swerved to the curb. The passenger door popped open as it stopped.

It was my client. "Get in," she called.

107

I lowered myself into the low-slung seat. The engine revved and we darted into traffic even as I tried without success to understand the seatbelt harness.

"Don't bother," my client said as she downshifted and the little car growled around a corner. Her hair was down and tumbled over her shoulders. "That belt is tangled, doesn't work. Haven't got to fixing it yet."

"You're restoring this?"

"Yep. You should have seen it two years ago when I found it. It's a lot of work, but I like working with my hands."

The gears protested as we took another corner. I noticed that the neighborhood had gotten sketchy.

"I thought we were going to the police."

She shot me a quick glance. "Yeah, about that. I think maybe you were right."

"Me? About what?"

"When you said the pictures could get leaked. I'd prefer not to let that happen."

We pulled up outside a rundown mid-century apartment building. Chiseled granite below the cornice proclaimed this was the Wickersham Place Apartments, and the address was Rich Rosenthal's. Although the street was on level ground, Brigid ratcheted the parking brake hard and then cramped the front wheels against the curb. Life in a city of hills makes those actions automatic. Only then did she meet my stare.

"I want you to help me cut a deal with him. I'm good at cutting deals. It's what I do for a living." She gestured at the street, lined with sad, rundown buildings. "I'm more used to board rooms and executive suites and can use your presence. I mean, you have a gun, don't you?

"A gun?"

She formed a pistol with her fingers. "You know, bang, bang?"

I flashed my coat. "Nope, no gun."

"Well, probably not needed."

I wondered if there was a trace of disappointment in her voice. "Let me go up first, scope things out, okay?" *And maybe call the cops*, I thought to myself.

"What, and leave me alone on this street? No thank you." She climbed out, her skirt granting me a generous view of shapely legs.

I got out and did what men have been doing since the dawn of time. I followed the lady.

*

As shabby apartment buildings go, the Wickersham wasn't so bad. No rats scurried past the baseboards, and the air was mostly breathable. Rosenthal's apartment was up three floors, but we took the stairs by mutual agreement. The rusting gates on the elevator didn't inspire the confidence that Mister Otis' name once engendered.

The hallway on the third floor was empty of people. We found Rosenthal's apartment and I knocked.

The unlatched door swung open on well-oiled hinges. The building must have been better cared for than I had been willing to give credit. It was an incongruous thought, given what sprawled on the floor in front of me. It was the body of a man, tall, thin and scruffy. He lay on his back and stared at the ceiling with lifeless eyes framed by wireframe glasses. His torso was soaked in blood; a bloody chest wound the source. The smell of gunpowder and death was strong. A simple job gets you every time.

I pulled Brigid into the apartment and closed the door. No reason to invite the rest of the world into the scene.

I knelt next to the body and held a finger to his neck. No pulse, not that I expected to find one. That was also the moment when I realized the woman standing behind me had quite a few reasons to see this man dead—twenty-five grand worth of reasons, every three months. She also carried a purse large enough to hold a good-sized pistol. Maybe even the same as the one that put a good-sized hole in Rosenthal's chest.

I stood up slowly and turned to face her. My relief at not facing a pistol must have been evident as her eyes narrowed.

"What? You thought—"

Her reply to my unvoiced suspicion was hushed before it began when we heard a toilet flush from somewhere inside the apartment. I pointed at the door. "Go out in the hallway, quick," I hissed. I took up a position flat against the wall where the hallway began, just in time to see Brigid duck behind a sofa in the tiny living room. There was a heavy table lamp within reach. I grabbed it and raised it over my head.

Whoever it was, they were taking their sweet time. I found myself staring at a Grateful Dead poster. The seconds ticked by and the lamp grew heavy.

Brigid stood up from behind the sofa. "Hey, jerk face," she shouted, then ducked back down.

I saw a shadow move on the hallway wall, and readied the lamp.

He came fast, and I had forgotten to unplug the lamp. The cord caught and deflected the lamp. He was raising his pistol when the lamp crashed down on his arm. The gun clattered to the floor and he knelt down to grab for it. I kicked it away, and then jumped on his back as he scrambled for the gun, knocking him flat on the floor. I pulled his arms up behind him.

That should have stopped him, but Paul, the clerk at the FedUps store, fought with the frenzy of a desperate man. Again and again he came near to slipping out of my grasp.

Fights in movies are accompanied by stirring music. Our fight was in silence, save for grunts, sharp breaths, and our shoes scuffing the floor.

A cocking pistol halted our fight and by unspoken consent we cast our eyes in that direction.

Brigid held Paul's gun in both hands, and she held it like she knew what she was doing. I couldn't tell if she was aiming at me or at Paul. I got the feeling he didn't know either. A long silence followed.

"Well, don't just lie there, you dope," she said at last. "You're the detective, not me. Tie the guy up or something and let's call the cops."

Not the sweetest phrase by any stretch, but a welcome one, all the same.

*

I stopped at the Double Tap Lounge the next evening. It's a bar down in Cow Hollow that caters to private detectives. I knew I was in for some ribbing from my colleagues and competition, and figured I might as well get it over with.

"You have got to be kidding." Jens shook his head in disbelief when I finished the story. "You let the perp razzle you?"

"I don't get it," complained Marty, who never got it. "How'd the FedUps guy get the photographs?"

"Rich Rosenthal was cleaning out his old files," I explained. "He was taking his photos in batches down to Paul's store to scan and save them on a data stick."

Marty nodded. "And Paul stole the stick. I get it."

"No. He hacked into the store's copier and was surfing images left on it by customers. He had been doing it for months. When he recognized Brigid Morgan's face in the photo, he knew he'd struck gold."

"And then our pal here," Jens slapped me on the back, a hefty, hearty slap. "Let the guy bamboozle him with one of the oldest dodges in the business."

"Okay." Marty nodded again. "I get that, I think. But why did he kill the photographer after putting the finger on him?"

"He figured if Rich were dead, the case would be closed." I gave a silent prayer that that was the last time I would have to tell the story.

"Alright, everybody, listen up." Jens' voice boomed through the room and brought a dozen conversations to silence. How a bearded, bald giant stayed the best undercover man in the business I never understood, but that was Jens.

"As you know, it is our custom at the Double Tap to assess a fine upon those of our trade who royally screw up." A ragged cheer came from all but me. "Accordingly, our friend will graciously buy a round on the house." Another cheer.

I stood, waved them quiet, then dropped a couple of century notes on the table. "That should cover the drinks." I made a show of checking the time. "But if you'll excuse me, ladies and gentlemen, I have a date to keep."

I tipped my hat and left to catcalls and jeers. Outside the Double Tap Lounge, a powder-blue TR6 idled next to the curb, the passenger door an open invitation.

Beautiful Killer
Judy Penz Sheluk

The whole of the Quick River is about three miles long and a few yards wide, an insignificant tributary that cuts through the heart of Quick County. Billy used to call it Speedy Creek.

It's been twenty years since I've been back, and at first glance not much has changed. The cluster of clapboard cabins dotting the Quick's rocky shoreline still need a good coat of fire, and the public dock still leans haphazardly to the left. Even the Quick 'n Slow Diner seems stuck in time, its chinked logs weather-beaten to a dull gray, the tables inside scarred by decades of hot plates and hard times.

The restaurant is empty, save for a thirty-something man I take to be the proprietor. The lack of customers doesn't surprise me. It's early April, too soon for rentals.

"Welcome. What brings you here on such a miserable day? GPS take a wrong turn?" The man says it with an easy smile. Something about him is familiar, but I can't stick a pin in it.

"My folks used to rent one of the cabins every season. I spent most of my summers here as a teenager." I grin, feel it tug on my lips like plastic surgery gone wrong. "It was longer ago than I care to admit."

"I knew it. You're Carly." He sticks out his hand, the skin roughened by years of washing dishes and peeling potatoes. "Dan Porter. Billy's kid brother. It's been a while."

"Danny...how did I miss it? You must think I've turned into one of those snooty city slickers from up at the Resort." I take his hand and study him. He's taller than I remember, a few pounds heavier, but he's got Billy's eyes. Black-rimmed gray flecked with blue.

"No worries. I've lost most of my hair since then." Danny runs his fingers through the thinning strands, pats his paunch, and laughs. "Put on some weight, too. You though, you haven't changed a bit. The years have been kind."

They haven't, but I don't answer. It doesn't seem right to reply with a glib remark about crow's feet and cellulite. Or tell the story of my somewhat pathetic life.

Danny stickhandles the moment with another easy smile. "You never did say. What brings you back?"

"I suppose I wanted to find myself again." Spoken out loud, the admission seems lame at best, sanctimonious at worst.

But Danny seems to accept it. "You want to talk? Coffee's on the house."

"I'm not sure where to start," I say, but pull up a seat overlooking the river.

Danny walks over to the front door, hangs a "Closed" sign in the window. "You still drink your coffee black?"

"You've got a good memory. What were you? Fifteen to my eighteen?"

"Something like that," he says, and a flash of embarrassment flickers across his face. "God, I had such a crush on you. Course, everyone knew you only had eyes for Billy."

"Billy." My heart ached at the memory of him. The way his fingers traced every vertebrae of my spine as I lay face down on the dock, the sun shimmering on my bronzed skin. The way his lips would part, ever so softly, just before he leaned down to kiss me. There was the rest of the world, and then there was Billy.

"He was the first boy to break my heart, did you know that? Dumped me a week before my eighteenth birthday. Didn't even stop by the cabin. Just phoned, said he was going around with Roxanne Reesor." I attempt a smile, as if the whole thing is barely remembered teenaged angst. "That's what we used to call having sex back then. Going around with each other. I wasn't ready. It cost me Billy."

"It wouldn't have mattered. Billy had a way of breaking hearts to keep his own intact. He used to say people got lost in love, but he wasn't going to be one of them. Bullshit, really, though I used to believe it. If it's any consolation, Billy broke up with Roxanne right after you left for school. She never got over him."

"I guess it shouldn't be, after all these years, but it kind of is. I like to imagine her dried up by bitterness and booze." I blush at the admission. "Roxanne never did bring out the best in me. I've often wondered what became of her."

"She married me. Any Porter in a storm." Danny's witticism is watered down by years in the telling; he looks out the window, self-conscious, his eyes scanning the river. "Roxanne was like the purple loosestrife that creeps along the shore of the Quick every summer. Tall, spiky stalks so lovely in bloom, yet destructive, relentless in its life-choking stranglehold. Takes hold and won't let go, the roots growing a foot deep and more. The beautiful killer, some folks call it." His fingers trace the rim of his coffee mug. "She left me fifteen years ago, come the tenth of July."

Fifteen years. I wonder at what point he'll stop marking the anniversary. "I'm sorry."

Danny looks deep into my eyes. His pain radiates, hot and raw and exposed, as if it's been simmering under the surface waiting for someone to come along and pick off the scab.

"I tried to stop her," he says, his voice breaking. "I was too late."

"You can't stop someone from leaving. Not if they want to go. You can't let it consume you." I say the words softly and wish I could follow my own advice.

"It's not that," Danny says, and gets up to flip the sign on the door to "Open." For the first time I notice the black marble plaque hanging next to the entrance, the words etched in gold leaf, a spiky stalk of flowers engraved into each corner.

In Memory of
WILLIAM (BILLY) PORTER
ROXANNE (REESOR) PORTER
Lost in Love
July 10, 2000

The Fruit of Thy Loins
Albert Tucher

Diana raised her fist to knock, but the door swung inward. That left her looking as if she planned to rap on the forehead of the young woman who confronted her in the doorway.

The idea had merit. Diana didn't need competition on her own territory. The other woman was in her early twenties, with eyes of a piercing blue. The eyes looked familiar, or maybe they just made a striking contrast with her dark hair and complexion.

She stepped back and held the door open.

"He's all yours."

Diana nodded minimal thanks and entered the motel room. There was her client Stephen on the bed. He showed no reaction to the little drama at the door, but many men noticed nothing that didn't hit them over the head.

Diana's hooker radar bleeped, and she looked again. Stephen had surrendered to gravity in a way that no living body could match.

She heard the door close, but that didn't mean the brunette was on the other side of it.

Instinct told Diana to spin to her right. Her hand chopped the other woman's wrist, and something fell onto the threadbare carpet. Diana completed her turn and threw a roundhouse left that shouldn't have had a chance.

But Diana's punch landed on the young woman's cheek and threw her off balance. Diana shoved with her right hand, and her opponent sat hard on the floor. She groped for what she had just dropped, but Diana brushed it under the bed with her foot and made a mental note to look when she had time.

Diana steadied herself and kicked. She missed, but she kept her balance for another try. This time her stiletto heel connected with the woman's jaw.

The brunette toppled onto her back and rolled onto her side. She drew her knees up to her chest, as if to protect herself from more punishment. But then her feet shot out and kicked Diana's legs out from under her.

Diana landed on her hip and pivoted to face her opponent, but the young woman only wanted to get away. She scrambled to her feet and lurched toward the exit. This time the door banged shut with the brunette on the outside.

Diana tried to get up, but her left knee had taken the brunt of the kick. It buckled and dumped her on the rug again. Outside, an engine roared, and tires shrieked.

She looked around for the item that had fallen. She expected a knife, but it turned out to be a nasty syringe. Diana thought about picking it up to examine it, but she didn't need the cops finding her fingerprints on it. It could stay where it was.

There had been a bag on the floor by the door, but the young woman had taken it on her way out. Diana remembered it as looking bigger than a basic receptacle for lube, wipes, condoms and a change of underwear.

She tried to get up again, and this time her knee cooperated. Her client still looked dead, and the syringe probably had something to do with it.

Next, she looked for a white envelope. If she found her money, the temptation would be hard to resist. But she knew who would be joining her soon, and he would not appreciate it if she interfered with his crime scene.

She found nothing on the flimsy table in the corner, on any of the counters in the bedroom or bathroom, or in the drawers of the bureau. The other woman must have taken the cash.

Murder and attempted murder were bad enough, but stealing from another hooker just wasn't done.

Diana picked up the room phone and dialed 9-1-1. She had done it before, but never with a clearer conscience.

First to arrive was a uniformed officer, who frisked her with professional detachment and told her to stand against the wall. He watched her as he got on his handheld radio. She let him finish.

"Is Breitwieser coming?"

The officer ignored her, but she had made her point. She knew Detective Breitwieser, and it would be prudent for the officer to treat her right.

The man himself arrived fifteen minutes later in all his combed-over glory. He had a new suit that was blue instead of brown, and not his usual polyester.

It was still a 46-regular, but progress was progress.

"Just once," said Breitwieser, "could I have a crime scene without you in the middle of it? Is that too much to ask?"

She let him vent. Their shared history might save her from going to the police station in handcuffs.

He turned to the uniformed officer.

"Get out there and start your crime scene log."

The young man looked disappointed. An ambitious uniformed officer would want to get in on the investigation, but he knew enough to keep his mouth shut and follow orders.

Breitwieser turned back to her. "Tell."

By now Diana knew that he liked his reports detailed. When she got to describing the young woman, she could sense his interest.

"Does that ring a bell?"

"It might," he said. "Did you know you were going to be changing shifts like that?"

"No, but it happens—a guy lining up dates back to back, or even back to back to back."

"You're okay with that?"

"Doesn't matter what I think. The client's money talks. Anyway, Stephen knew the rules. He would have tipped me. Not the same as a two-hour date, but worth swallowing my pride."

"But your money walked."

She shrugged. Breitwieser nodded at the syringe on the floor.

"How did she get him to hold still for that?"

"She had a bag. Bigger than mine, which tells me she was carrying fetish gear or a costume. If I had to guess, I'd say she was doing a nurse act."

Someone knocked on the door, and the uniformed officer opened and poked his head inside.

"Crime scene guys are here, Detective."

"Let's take a ride to the station," said Breitwieser. "Got something to show you."

That was not good news. She had always avoided the Morristown station. But on the other hand, he made no move to cuff her, and in the parking lot he opened the passenger door and held it for her.

She did know a few other cop shops, and this one offered no surprises. When they arrived, he led her to a room with a video monitor and pointed at a plain plastic chair behind a table. He looked around the room.

"Shit," he said. He went to the door and bellowed, "Who's got the fucking remote this time?"

Diana pulled the chair out from the table and stopped herself from sitting on something that didn't belong there. "Here it is."

He took the remote from her and turned the monitor on. A moment later a brief video clip played. It showed a woman walking away from an expensive yacht. The camera had a poor angle. By looking down at her feet, the woman concealed her face.

But her movements were familiar, and so was the yacht behind her.

"Could that be her?" asked Breitwieser.

"Definitely."

"How can you be sure?"

"The way she moves. You fight with somebody, you get to know her."

"That's from the shore, obviously. The cops down there are circulating this."

"The rich guy who OD'ed. Duane Antonelli."

"He was from around here. And you remember his name."

She knew she had to tell him. It was going to come out sooner or later. "He was a client."

"That's interesting."

"I don't really see how, but I thought I'd better tell you. I spent an afternoon on his boat a couple of weeks ago."

"I guess he invited her, too. And she thanked him by helping him OD."

"Any idea who she is?"

"Not unless she showed you her driver's license before she tried to stick you."

He looked at her for a long moment, and she could see his mind working. A lot of people might have been fooled into seeing a dull, plodding cop, but she wasn't one of them. He knew the young hooker would be coming for her. Diana was a living witness.

"You understand we can't put surveillance on you. We don't have the manpower."

"You'd just kill my business, anyway."

"The best we can do is have your local guys drive by as often as possible."

She smiled as she thought of the police in her hometown of Driscoll babysitting a hooker.

"No, I'm wrong," he said. "The best we can do is find her fast."

"Sounds good to me."

"Okay," he said. "I'll get a uniform to drive you back to your car."

The officer wasn't feeling talkative, which was fine with her. She had some thinking to do.

Her first idea was to spread the word in the online discussion groups for women in the business. But she dismissed that. It took references to get access, but at some point the woman could have fooled someone.

Working the phone would take more time, but it was the only way to go.

The first call was to Mary Alice Mercier, aka Crystal, Diana's closest friend in the business, after they had settled a few differences. It was a long story.

She told Mary Alice about the bad date with Stephen.

"Damn," said Mary Alice. "When are you going to learn and stop going down to Morristown?"

It wasn't a real question. Mary Alice knew that hookers went where the money was.

"She's going to come for me," said Diana. "I want to get it over with. So if somebody asks, go ahead and tell her. She's the kind who doesn't have friends, and it would never occur to her that you might warn me."

Nothing happened for twenty-four nerve-wracking hours. Even clients stayed away. That happened sometimes, and she didn't usually fret. But this time it was hard to avoid imagining the young brunette methodically slaughtering them.

Then Mary Alice called back.

"I got a bad feeling. Bitch."

"What?"

"Not you. The cat won't stop climbing on me."

"You don't have a cat."

"I do for the next three weeks. You remember my neighbor, Fred? Cute young guy?"

"Vaguely."

"He dumped her on me while he's away. Cats can tell when you hate them, and they're all over you."

Mary Alice was always letting cute guys impose on her. Sometimes it even cut into her business. Diana never let that happen, but now wasn't the time to lecture her friend.

"So what's this bad feeling about?"

"Victoria. I tried getting in touch with her about this thing, but she's not answering her personal cell or her email. And she's always on the discussion group, but not a peep for a couple of days now."

"Would she know how to find me?"

"I might have mentioned something," said Mary Alice. "I know I told her some of your regular clients. Just to give her the lay of the land. I mentioned Stephen, matter of fact."

"So that bitch might have gotten to her."

They listened to each other's breathing.

"I'm here for the afternoon," said Mary Alice. "I'll keep trying her."

It was against Diana's hooker religion to initiate contact with the cops, but Breitwieser needed to know this. She made the call.

"Interesting," he said. "You know this Victoria?"

"I've seen her in a couple of parking lots. She's just starting out, and she's older than most newbies."

She heard tapping on a keyboard.

"Well, look here. Her real name is Sallie Antonelli."

That didn't surprise Diana. Cops always knew who was doing her kind of work. A uniformed officer saw the same car parked at several motels and somebody ran the license plate.

"Makes me think, ex-wife," said Breitwieser. "Maybe a bad pre-nup left her hurting financially."

"That would make sense. Mary Alice probably knows the story. They've talked."

"Oh, God."

"She's not your biggest fan, either. If you want, I'll ask her."

"Let's do it that way to start with. I can concentrate on looking for Sallie."

Diana hung up and felt cabin fever closing in on her. She decided to use her feet instead of the phone. Mary Alice lived just a dozen blocks away in an apartment over a barber shop in downtown Driscoll.

The walk appealed at the moment, and if that blue-eyed psycho was lurking on the way, they would settle this thing. But nothing happened to get her adrenaline working.

The entrance to the residential second floor was around the side of the building. Diana rang the doorbell and waited.

Nothing happened. She swore and then scolded herself. Mary Alice could go out on the spur of the moment if she wanted.

But then the door buzzed. Diana pushed it open and started climbing. At the top of the stairs she knocked on the door to the apartment. It opened. She stepped inside.

"Oh," she said.

The young woman in Mary Alice's kitchen wasn't Mary Alice, but she looked familiar, even without a syringe in her hand. A gun had taken its place.

"I learn from experience," said the young woman.

"What's your name?"

"Roxanne. March."

"Roxanne March. I'll remember you."

"March, as in get moving."

Roxanne nodded toward Mary Alice's living room, where Diana had been a few times.

Mary Alice sat on her aging sofa against the far wall. Next to her was a blonde woman in her forties. Diana looked at the woman and knew where she had seen Roxanne's pale blue eyes before.

"Sallie. You're her mother."

"Right," said Roxanne. "And you're thinking I'm a second-generation whore."

"Give me a chance, and I wouldn't think about you at all."

"Well, I'm not a whore. I don't fuck anybody for money, and I wasn't about to fuck my stepfather at all."

She gave a nasty grin.

"He had a different idea. I wonder where he got it."

"Duane Antonelli. So what did you have against Stephen?"

Roxanne gave her a contemptuous look.

"Oh," said Diana. "You used him to get at me. I guess you really aren't a whore, because you don't get it. I'm not the other woman. It was just business."

"I don't care. I take care of my mother."

"I can see what a great job you do."

"I talked him into writing her a nice check. You'd think she'd be a little bit grateful."

Diana glanced at Sallie, who sat there with a stunned look on her face.

A phrase came into Diana's mind, something biblical from way back in her Sunday school days. "The fruit of thy loins."

Sallie was contemplating the fruit of her loins and wondering how she had gone so wrong. She also looked as if she had given up hope.

Mary Alice seemed to have more presence of mind, but she was leaving it to Diana to get something started.

"You going to shoot us?" said Diana. "That's not going to fool anybody."

"I still have my syringe. My mother will inject both of you."

"Not much of a choice for us."

"How's this? If you hold still and cooperate, somebody might even find you in time. If I have to shoot, I'll make damn sure you're dead."

Movement down at floor level caught Diana's eye. Mary Alice's cat for three weeks looked unimpressed by the drama around her. She went straight to Roxanne and started rubbing herself against the young woman's legs in their distressed jeans.

"Get away," said Roxanne.

The cat ignored her. Roxanne hooked her right foot under the cat's ribcage and heaved the animal toward Diana. The cat rolled in mid-air and landed on her feet.

"Shit, I hate cats."

So did I, Diana thought. *Until now.* She stooped and scooped up the cat. In the same motion she flung the beast back at Roxanne's face. The cat screeched and extended her claws.

Roxanne raised her left arm to protect her face. Her gun hand dropped to her side. She managed to parry the flying cat, but then Diana was right on top of her. Diana put everything behind her right elbow, as she drove it into Roxanne's face.

Roxanne's head snapped back. Diana grabbed her right wrist with both hands and twisted. The gun fell to the floor. Diana didn't want to let go of Roxanne, and she didn't have to. Mary Alice launched herself from the sofa and dove for the gun. She scrambled to her feet and backed up. To give Mary Alice a clear shot, Diana shoved Roxanne away from her.

"Sit," said Mary Alice. "There."

With her free hand she pointed at the space she had vacated on the sofa. Roxanne hesitated, but Mary Alice could look pretty scary when she needed to. Roxanne decided to obey. She sat next to her mother, who edged away. The younger woman touched her nose and looked at the blood on her fingers.

"That's better," said Diana.

The cat was sitting in the corner and licking a paw. Diana went and picked her up, which the cat tolerated.

"Pretty girl. What's your name?"

"Jezebel," said Mary Alice.

"Sweet," said Diana. "One of us."

The Raymond Chandler Con
Earl Staggs

Harry Phillips sat at his desk thinking murder was not supposed to happen in a small town like Sentry, Texas. That's why he moved here and took the job of Police Chief after twenty years as a cop in Dallas, where murder happened every other day.

His Chief Deputy, Pete Wilson, and two others were still at the home of the victim, Martha Robinson, processing the scene. Harry had gone there with them when the call came in first thing that morning. It was nearly noon, and he was anxious for their report.

A minute later, his secretary, Glenda, buzzed him. "Harry, there's someone here to see you. She says it's important."

Harry groaned. He had a homicide to work on. He didn't have time to listen to a complaint about someone's SUV blocking someone else's driveway or someone's cat raiding someone's garbage can.

"Send her in."

When she entered his office, Harry stood and invited her to sit by his desk. "How can I help you?"

She was short and heavyset and wore jeans, white sneakers, a Cowboys tee shirt, and thick glasses. She hadn't taken any pains with her short brown hair or makeup that morning, and her eyes looked swollen like she'd done a lot of crying.

"Chief Phillips," she said. "I'm Beth Harding. My best friend, Martha Robinson, was murdered last night. I know who did it."

Harry knew where this conversation was going. It was common after a killing. People always came forward to turn in the evil culprit who happened to be someone they hated and wanted to get even with for something. He had to humor them. It went with the job.

"I'm very sorry you lost a friend, Ms. Harding, but who do you think did it?"

"It was Richard Jennings."

"What makes you so sure it was him?"

"Martha dated him a couple times. He was nice enough at first, but she soon learned he was vulgar and mean and drank too much. She broke it off about a month ago, but he wouldn't leave her alone. He harassed her and stalked her. Everywhere she went, she'd see that big red pickup of his. I told her to get a restraining order against him, but she wouldn't do anything like that. She didn't want to get anybody in trouble."

"We'll certainly check him out, Ms. Harding. Do you know where he lives?"

"In Keller."

Harry buzzed Glenda. "Glenda, call Keller P.D. and see if you can get anything on a Richard Jennings." He thought this would satisfy Ms. Harding that he was taking her seriously.

She looked at him with wide, slightly reddened eyes. "Can't you just go arrest him?"

"I'm afraid not." Harry smiled across his desk. "Ms. Harding—"

"Please. Call me Beth."

"Okay, Beth, thank you for coming in with this information. We will definitely talk to him." He stood up, expecting her to do the same.

She didn't. "That could be a mistake, Harry. If he knows he's a suspect, he could skip to South America or somewhere." Her voice weakened. She reached in her pocket for a tissue and wiped her eyes. After a moment, she clinched the tissue in a fist and continued. "Are you familiar with Raymond Chandler?"

"One of our best crime writers."

"The very best, as far as I'm concerned. I remember a short story of his, one of his Philip Marlowe ones, with a situation like this one. Marlowe knew who the killer was, but he had no proof. He conned the guy into a confession."

"How did he do that?"

"He told the guy he witnessed the murder and would go to the police unless the guy paid him ten thousand dollars. The guy paid him, which was the same as a confession."

Harry grinned. "That might work in fiction, but not necessarily in real life. Besides, there are a lot of legal issues involved in something like that. I'd have to assign an officer to work undercover and—""You don't have to assign anyone. I'll do it."

"I can't let you do something like that. You're not a trained police officer. I can't put you in a dangerous situation like that."

"There wouldn't be any danger. You'd be close by to make sure of that. I've read everything Chandler wrote, Harry. Twice. And I watch every crime show on TV. In fact, I'm thinking about becoming a private detective. I can do this. You'll see."

Harry groaned inside. Just what he needed, another amateur P.I. running around loose. "I'm sorry, Beth, but it's out of the question. Reading books and watching TV do not qualify someone to be a detective. As soon as our preliminary investigation is done, we'll begin checking out suspects, and Mr. Jennings will be one of them."

She sat up straight and rigid in her chair. "Is that all you're going to do?"

"I'm sorry, but that's the best we can do for now. Please leave your phone number with my secretary, and we'll let you know when we come up with something."

She stood up abruptly. "Certainly, Chief Phillips, I'll do that," she said as she left

his office.

Harry didn't miss the trace of anger in her voice, and that she was not calling him Harry anymore. He hoped she wouldn't do anything foolish.

An hour later, Deputy Pete Wilson came into Harry's office. "Harry, we dusted all the usual places in the house for prints and DNA traces and came up with nothing. Even the doorknobs have been wiped clean. No sign of the murder weapon either. Her purse is missing and there's an empty jewelry case in the bedroom, so robbery could be the motive."

"Or it could be personal, and he only wanted it to look like a robbery."

"True. We canvassed the neighborhood and didn't get much. Guy across the street noticed a red pickup cruising the block several times in the last couple weeks, including last night. Could be something, could be nothing, but that's all we got. I stopped by the M.E.'s office and he drew a blank too. No traces on the body."

"Did the neighbor happen to get the plate number on that red pickup?"

"No, he wasn't close enough." Harry's intercom buzzed.

"Harry, here's what I came up with on Richard Jennings," Glenda said. "He's no stranger to Keller P.D. He's had three arrests for barroom brawling and lost his license twice for D.W.I.s. There were two arrests for physical abuse against women, but the charges were dropped both times. Keller is sure he paid them off. Interesting?"

"Very interesting."

"There's more. Keller considers him their worst nightmare—a low-class redneck with money. His parents left him a few hundred prime acres, which he promptly sold to a developer for a healthy fortune. He not only has low morals and bad habits, but plenty of money to indulge them. I went a step further and checked with motor vehicles. He drives a red Dodge pickup, and I have his license number if you want it."

"A red pickup, huh? Thanks, Glenda." Harry hung up and spoke to Pete Wilson. "Let's bring Richard Jennings in for questioning. Glenda has his address."

*

Pete Wilson called in at two o'clock. "No luck with Richard Jennings. No one here at his house, and his neighbors said he has no set schedule, just comes and goes at all hours."

130

"Thanks, Pete. Sit tight in case he shows up. I'll get a BOLO out on his vehicle."

After he'd arranged for the Be On the Look Out notice, Harry worked at his desk until six thirty. Still no sign of Richard Jennings at his home, and no results from the BOLO.

When the phone rang, Harry answered. Beth Harding said in a matter-of-act tone, "Harry, if you want proof against Richard Jennings, be at Moe's Diner on Denton Highway at nine tonight."

Big red alarm signals went off in Harry's gut. "Beth, what have you done?"

"I called him and told him I saw him coming out of Martha's house late last night. I said I wouldn't tell the police if he paid me a hundred thousand dollars. He agreed to do it. I'll have a tape recorder in my purse, and we'll get his confession when he pays me the money."

"Dammit, Beth, I told you to stay out of it and let us do our job. I can't allow you to put yourself in danger."

"Just be there, Harry. Nine o'clock. Don't be late."

Before he could protest further, she hung up.

Harry rushed out to Glenda's desk, found the phone number Beth had left and dialed it quickly. A recorded message came on in her voice.

The message was, "Moe's Diner on Denton Highway, Harry. Nine o'clock."

"Damn! Damn! Damn!"

Harry paced back and forth, his anger building. After a few minutes, he dropped in Glenda's chair. Beth had put herself in grave danger and he had to do something about it.

After a few more minutes of sitting and calming down, he thought, *What if she's right? What if Jennings is willing to admit his guilt by paying her off? It's crazy and it's risky, but if it worked for Raymond Chandler....*

*

At eight fifteen, Harry knocked on Beth Harding's front door.

"Harry," she said, "I said Moe's Diner at nine."

"Beth, we have to talk now."

Once they were seated at her dining room table, Harry jumped right into it.

"Beth, what you've done is crazy and dangerous. I could arrest you for interfering in a murder investigation."

"Well, since you weren't going to do anything, I decided to take matters into my own hands. If you want to arrest me, go ahead. You'll just be letting a murderer get away."

Harry sighed. "I'm not going to arrest you. Not yet anyway. We're going to play it out your way and see what happens. If it blows up in our faces, I'll lock you up and swallow the key."

He glared at her and he was sure she was suppressing a grin.

She managed to hold a straight face and asked, "How do you want to play it, Harry?"

"All right, listen carefully. When you get to the diner, the waitress will seat you in the last booth on the left. She's really one of my deputies, and she'll be armed. She'll seat me two booths in back of you. I've wired your booth for sound so I'll hear everything the two of you say. I'll have another deputy outside in an unmarked car. As soon as Jennings pays you the money, we'll step in and arrest him. Got that so far?"

"Got it."

"Good. One more thing, and this is very important. Everything takes place in the diner. Under no circumstances do you go outside with him. Got that?"

"Got it all, Harry."

*

At eight forty-five, Harry pulled in at Moe's Diner and drove around the building. The diner sat between two taller buildings, leaving a narrow canyon-like parking area on each side. He passed Pete Wilson sitting in his car on the north side of the diner and nodded. He did not see a red pickup.

Harry parked on the south side and went into the restaurant. Beth Harding was already seated in the last booth on the left. She sat facing him and looked in his direction, but made no sign of recognition. Deputy Peggy Randall approached him with a smile, looking every bit like a diner waitress, and escorted him to his booth. A dozen or so tables and booths were occupied by other patrons. Harry ordered a cup of coffee and pretended to study the menu.

At ten minutes past nine, Harry heard Pete Wilson's voice coming through his ear plug.

Pete said, "Incoming."

A tall, overweight man entered the diner. His faded jeans were too tight, his NASCAR tee shirt was wrinkled beyond recovery, and the baseball cap he wore to contain a wild mass of black hair was so old it was shapeless. He ignored Peggy, spotted the only female sitting alone, and walked toward Beth in the last booth on the left.

The first voice Harry heard was Beth's.

"Did you bring the money?"

"Yeah, I brought the money, but damned if I know what the hell for. You said you saw me last night, and it would cost me a hundred grand. Why don't you stop playing games and tell me what you're up to."

"Sure, I'll tell you, Mr. Jennings. I was across the street from Martha Robinson's house last night, and I saw you come out of there in a big hurry."

"Hey, lady, I don't know what you been smokin', but I didn't kill that woman."

"Yes you did. You killed her, and if you don't pay me a hundred thousand dollars, I'll tell the police."

"You're crazy, woman. You can't prove nothin'. It's your word against mine."

"Very well, Mr. Jennings, if that's the way you want it. I'll call the police right now, and we'll see who they believe."

"No! Wait! How do I know if I pay you, you won't still call the police? What guarantee do I get?"

"You'll get my word that I'll never say anything to anybody, not ever. Besides, I've always wanted to live in Europe. Your money is all I'll need to move there and get a new start. You'll never see or hear from me again."

"I guess I'll have to trust you," he said.

"I'm glad we agree, Mr. Jennings. Now, where's my money?"

"Out in my truck. Let's take a walk out there and get it."

"Oh, I'll just stay here while you get it."

"No, you have to go with me. I ain't takin' no chances on somebody seein' me pay you off."

Harry wanted to shout, *"Don't go, Beth!"* but it was too late. She was already following Jennings toward the door.

Harry waited until they were outside before he left his own booth. He caught Peggy Randall's eye and pointed toward the back of the restaurant. She understood and headed toward the entrance to the kitchen, which would get her to the rear exit. When Harry stepped outside, he saw Beth and Jennings turn the corner of the restaurant into the north parking area. Good. That's where Pete Wilson was parked.

"Coming to you, Pete," Harry said into his lapel mic. "Be ready."

"Ten four, Chief."

There were two rows of parking spots between the restaurant and the tall warehouse next door. Jennings' truck sat halfway down the back row, three cars up from Pete Wilson's spot, under a large fluorescent street light. Harry crouched and moved around the corner, staying lower than the cars parked in the first row. He stopped twenty feet from Jennings' truck and kept out of sight.

Jennings opened the driver's door of his truck. "Okay," he said. "Get in."

"No," Beth said. "Just give me my money and we're done."

Jennings reached under his shirt, pulled a hunting knife from his waistband, and held it against Beth's rib cage. "Get in the truck. You think I'm stupid? I pay you, you just go through it and come back for more. Get in. We're goin' for a little ride."

Harry drew his gun and stood up. "Police!" he shouted. "Richard Jennings, you're under arrest. Drop the knife."

Jennings spun Beth around in front of him and threw his free arm around her waist, still pressing the knife against her side.

Harry shouted again. "Drop the knife! Now!"

Jennings glowered at him and shook his head. "Back off, cop. I ain't goin' to prison. I'll do her right here."

Harry whispered into his mic. "Pete, shoot the light over his head."

The BANG! from Pete's Glock echoed like a bomb between the buildings. Instantly, the fluorescent light overhead exploded in a blinding flash, and a shower of sparks spewed to the ground.

The distraction caused Jennings to loosen his grip on Beth, and she fell to her hands and knees by his side. Harry moved toward them, his gun extended in both hands. "Drop the knife, Jennings, or the next shot goes through your head."

Jennings took only a second to toss his knife to the ground.

Harry moved closer. "You okay, Beth?"

"I'm fine." She rose to her feet and brushed at her knees. "But I think I'll have bruises."

*

The next morning at eleven, Beth came to the station and gave her statement about the night before. As soon as she finished, she hurried to Harry's office.

"Good morning," she said.

"Good morning, Beth. How are your bruises?"

"Not as bad as I thought."

"Good. You'll be happy to know, last night we charged Jennings with assaulting you with a deadly weapon."

Her eyes narrowed. "Assault? Didn't you listen to his murder confession on the tape?"

"We listened, and it's all there. Unfortunately, a smart lawyer could challenge it as being inconclusive and inadmissible."

"What are you saying? Jennings could get away with killing Martha?"

Harry chuckled. "Relax, Beth. He's not going to get away with anything. I was just giving you a hard time. Serves you right for what you put me through last night. We searched his truck and found his bloody clothes wadded up under the front seat. We also found Martha's wallet and jewelry, and traces of blood on his knife. I'm sure the lab will tell us it was Martha's. He was smart enough to wipe the crime scene clean, but not smart enough to get rid of the evidence right away. At nine o'clock this morning, we charged him with the murder of Martha Robinson."

Beth plopped into a chair. "Well, that's a relief."

"And, I have more good news for you. I'm not going to arrest you for interfering with a police investigation."

She smiled. "Thank you for that, Harry."

"On one condition."

"What's that?'

"We might never have caught Jennings without you, and we're grateful to you for what you did. You were very brave, and I know

Raymond Chandler would be proud of you. But, you have to promise me you'll never do anything like that again."

She gave him a wide grin. "I can't promise you, Harry, but I'll try."

The Wrong Girl
Barb Goffman

I was replacing a roll of toilet paper in the handicapped stall when the restroom door banged open. My cart had pushed the stall door slightly ajar, so I could see a thin blond girl lean against the sink, breathing hard, eyes tearing.

Poor child.

The bathroom door crashed open again. A redhead and a brunette rushed in. All three girls wore the same tight jeans and had iron-straight hair.

"Are you okay?" Ginger squeezed Blondie's arm.

Blondie shook her off. "Mrs. Zulkowitz is such a bitch!"

"She totally is," Cocoa said.

"I hate her," Blondie said. "Hate. Her."

I'd been a janitor at this private school for nearly thirty years, and I'd heard this sentiment more than once. Paula Zulkowitz taught fifth grade. She was known for being strict and domineering, her tongue as sharp as the crease in her trousers. Over the years, she'd made many children cry. I'd seen and heard them weeping in the halls and bathrooms, though these rich children never noticed me. Like now.

"I can't believe she did that," Ginger said. "Making you go to the front of the room to read a passage, and then interrupting you after every single word. So rude."

"Public speaking is totally overrated," Cocoa said. "So what if you talk too fast?"

"I don't talk too fast," Blondie yelled, her words jumbling into each other. She totally talked too fast.

"Well, it's over now," Ginger said. "When you stormed out of the room, Mrs. Z let us go for lunch. Only six minutes late."

"Oh, it's not over." Blondie wiped tears off her cheek. "She's messed with the wrong girl. We have to do something."

"Like what?" Cocoa asked.

Blondie sniffed and pulled lip gloss from her pocket. She rubbed the shiny pink wand over her lips perfectly without looking in the mirror. Ginger and Cocoa quickly grabbed their gloss and started primping too.

"You remember how Mrs. Z is allergic to hand sanitizer?" Blondie said. "Tomorrow when she's not looking, we'll rub and spray it all over the classroom. Especially the markers for that stupid whiteboard she loves so much."

"Ooh, and her desk," Cocoa joined in. "And her chair. She touches them a lot."

Blondie nodded. "And that big dictionary she flips through every day, teaching us a new word, like we're stupid or something."

"But she'll get sick," Ginger said. "That's why she told us at the beginning of the year we couldn't bring any hand sanitizer to school. Ever. She's deathly allergic."

"Exactly." Blondie smiled. Ginger pursed her lips, looking nervous. Blondie glared at her. "You have a problem?"

Blinking a few times, Ginger shook her head. "No." Her voice trembled.

"Good," Blondie said. "We'll do it first thing tomorrow, when she leaves to get her precious mug of coffee. Now c'mon. Let's go to lunch."

She smoothed her hair and practically pranced out of the room, her minions in her wake.

It wasn't the first time I'd heard kids plot against their teachers. Usually they were simply blowing off steam. But sometimes, like now, I could tell the kids meant it. In the past, I'd reported them to the principal. The result every time: parents were summoned, the children pleaded they'd been joking, and the incidents were swept under the rug. No punishments. No consequences.

Not this time. Mean girls who faced no consequences grew up to become mean women who thought they could bully everyone and get away with everything. I couldn't let that happen again. This time, I'd let the plan move forward far enough that the authorities would have to act.

Finally, justice would be served.

*

Right before the school doors opened the next morning, I spilled a bucket full of water outside Mrs. Zulkowitz's classroom. I'd just begun mopping up when the kids streamed into the building. Blondie walked by with her friends, smirking. The plan was on.

I maneuvered myself so I could see into the classroom without being obvious. Mrs. Zulkowitz was writing an assignment on the whiteboard as the kids emptied their backpacks. She then grabbed her mug and headed to the teachers' lounge at the end of the hall. She didn't say a word to me.

Blondie and her pals went immediately to work, spritzing and rubbing hand sanitizer everywhere. A few kids were watching, wide-eyed, but they didn't interfere. Blondie clearly was too powerful.

Moments later Mrs. Zulkowitz emerged from the teachers' lounge, sipping from her mug. I stepped toward her. It was time to act. The girls couldn't pretend they'd been joking now.

"Excuse me, I need to—"

"Aaah!" Mrs. Zulkowitz slipped in the puddle. Her body slammed onto the floor, the coffee splashing her as the mug shattered.

"Oh, God." I dropped my mop and ran to her. "Let me help you."

"You idiot! What kind of moron allows water to sit out like this?"

I wanted to point out the bright yellow "danger, wet floor" caution boards I'd set out, but the woman clearly was in pain. "I'm so sorry. Are you okay?"

"Do I look okay?" Mrs. Zulkowitz ignored my extended hand and stood, wringing her silk shirt. "My blouse is ruined. I might have burns on my stomach. And I'll be bruised for a week."

"I'll pay the dry-cleaning bill." I couldn't afford it, but since I'd purposely spilled that water, it was the least I could do.

"You're damn right you will." She stepped toward her classroom.

"Wait. I need to—"

"I'm done speaking with you, you imbecile."

"But—"

"Just shut up. I'll have you fired for this, you incompetent boob."

My face grew hot as she marched into her classroom and reached for a sanitized whiteboard marker.

I let her.

Silent Measures
BV Lawson

Scott Drayco knew the statistics were grim—if kidnap victims weren't found in a week, chances they'd turn up alive dwindled fast. The police weren't giving up on the case, but the child's mother didn't have much faith left. Not after the ransom was delivered, but the boy wasn't returned. Three weeks and not a word.

The father of Joey Jensen wasn't on board with hiring a private consultant until his wife's insistence wore him down. Grim statistics or no, Drayco gladly took on the case, unable to get the mother's tear-stained face out of his mind. After preliminary interviews with the family's friends and foes, he had a snapshot of the situation that got clearer by the day. But definitely not any prettier.

The father was essentially a modern-day carpetbagger, buying up properties at bargain-basement prices from desperate homeowners after floods and hurricanes, and selling them to developers for a tidy profit. It hadn't won him many friends.

The mother was well-intentioned, but trying to keep up with the high-society Joneses meant a parade of babysitters and boarding schools for a boy who crimped her lifestyle. Especially a boy who was deaf.

The teachers at Keirnes Boarding School where Joey disappeared were polite, but defensive. Perhaps because a few of the students confided to Drayco that Joey was often disciplined in "the box room" for misbehaving. When Drayco saw the box room, a space about the size of a walk-in closet with bare walls and one lonely seat in a corner, he thought Joey might have run away, the kidnapping all a hoax. Until Drayco heard a tape of the ransom phone call.

The voice on the phone was digitally altered in a professional way hard for a deaf child to do. And then there was the mysterious series of bangs at the end of the call. Joey's mother was terrified the banging was a gun, but Drayco's expert ears knew better. The synesthete part of his brain also picked up on something else, some color and texture of that sound he felt he should be able to identify.

The most helpful witness was one of Joey's boarding schoolmates, a nine-year-old named Chase Cole. Like Joey, Chase had a cochlear implant, giving him muted hearing and the ability for limited speech. When Drayco asked Chase about Joey's habits, Chase said Joey liked to haunt the musical therapy room. Joey especially enjoyed putting hands inside the piano when someone was playing, to feel the vibrations.

The musical therapy room was in the north wing of the school, and Joey walked there through an outdoor trail every evening at seven, come rain, ice or snow. Many school staff knew this, but it would be easy for an outside kidnapper to pinpoint the perfect time and place to snatch the child.

As Drayco now stood on that trail with Assistant Principal Jennifer Stott, who was also one of the music teachers, he saw how isolated the trail really was. Unfortunately, the staff and police who'd trampled through the area long ago obliterated any signs of Joey or his kidnapper.

Drayco pointed to a door on the east wing of the school. "So Joey's room was over there, and he'd use that exit to walk to the music room?" Drayco pivoted north, "Up there."

Jennifer nodded. "That's right. Every day without fail."

"Why that time, at seven?"

"That's when I give the more hearing-abled students piano lessons."

"But not Joey?"

"Most of my piano students weren't born deaf, but developed hearing loss later. Children with congenital deafness like Joey have a much harder time. He tries to play, bless his dear soul, but he just can't quite hear well enough. He really loves it when I play Beethoven. I don't know if it's the music, or the fact I told him Beethoven lost his hearing."

"Beethoven's one of my favorites, too."

"Do you play?"

"From time to time." Drayco motioned toward the north wing and said, "Shall we?"

It only took three minutes to walk the path, even littered as it was with slick red and orange leaves following a recent rain. The music room turned out to be in the corner of the north wing—the closest room to a two-lane road forming one of the school's boundaries. Very convenient for someone wanting to grab the boy and whisk him away in a car.

They entered the building and made their way into the music room. In one corner, castanets, triangles and drums jockeyed for position on a table. Along one wall, a row of tall shelves was crammed with instrument cases for trumpets, violins and flutes. The piano was front and center, like a maestro ready to whip the other instruments into shape.

Drayco fingered the lid of the Steinway. "What can you tell me about Joey's parents?" When he saw her biting her lip, he added, "Strictly off the record."

Drayco's companion sank onto the piano bench, facing him. "I do believe Mrs. Jensen really loves little Joey. It's just…" Jennifer sighed. "She's clueless about how to be a mother. I suppose it's to be expected, her being an orphan and all. Went through the foster system—not many good role models. But she does love him, I'm certain of it."

"And Joey's father?"

"Sometimes I think if it were a choice between his son and money, he'd take the money."

"Yet he paid the ransom."

"He had to, didn't he? It would have looked bad, if he hadn't."

"Mr. Jensen's business seems a perfect motive-maker for people wanting revenge. Had there been threats against Joey you're aware of?"

"Here at the school?"

"Especially here at the school."

"None I've heard." She hesitated before adding, "But there was something odd."

The hairs prickled at the back of Drayco's neck. "Odd in what way?"

"It sounds like a child's fancies. Most children are afraid of the dark, monsters under the bed, that kind of thing."

Drayco waited patiently, as Jennifer rubbed her shoe over a frayed thread in the checkerboard carpeting. "Joey said he thought someone was looking in his window at night. He's on the first floor, so it's not impossible. To humor him, we checked the ground under his window, but didn't see anything out of the ordinary. Then later, he thought someone entered his room and stood next to his bed. He was frightened, even ducked under the covers."

"So no description of this mystery visitor?"

"If he exists at all. The school's psychologist thinks it's a cry for attention."

"Is this the same psychologist who thinks Joey ran away?"

Jennifer frowned. "The same."

"You don't agree, I take it?"

"He's an impressionable little boy, I'll give you that."

Drayco recalled the box room and tried to stem the flash of anger that image aroused. "Seems like putting an impressionable little boy in the box room would be a bad idea."

She looked at the floor and kicked harder at the loose thread. "I'm not a fan of the box room. But I get out-voted every time the subject comes up about doing away with it."

"Whose idea was it?"

"It was here before I came. This is only my second term, you see. I think it's been used as punishment off and on for three years."

"Was Joey the only child put in the box room?"

146

"Now that you mention it, I think so, yes."

Drayco stared at her. "Were Joey's parents aware of this punishment?"

"I'm not sure. They knew he'd been having some problems. I don't think they felt it was anything to worry over."

Jennifer looked at her watch. "I hate to rush things, but I have an appointment in the office in ten minutes."

Drayco pointed to the piano on their way out. "You said Joey tried to play that piano but couldn't hear well enough. Surely the cochlear implants helped."

"It helped some. But take one clumsy-fingered child who's also partially deaf and you get a lot of ugly banging."

Drayco thanked her for her time and told her he was going to take a walk around the property. Beside the road border on the north, and the main building to the east, the school shared two borders with other landowners. One owner was a farmer who grew mostly hay and kept a few cows, while the other was one of the school's English teachers. Both had fences to mark the property lines, and both fences were electrified. Joey couldn't have climbed over, unless the juice was turned off.

Drayco smiled at the thought of the little boy happily banging out music on the keyboard. And then the synesthete clues percolating just under his conscious mind bubbled to the surface.

After hurrying back to his car, he hopped inside and pulled out his laptop. He listened to the copy of the original audio file from the ransom phone call again. Next, he opened the file in his forensic software. He'd already tried using some basic reverse transforms to I.D. the voice, but the end result was a garbled mess.

This time, he paid closer attention to the banging. He slowed the audio down as much as he could, and made out not one bang, but a series of bangs. Four in all. The police thought it was car noises in the background, but he didn't think so. The sounds were more like notes. Notes that sounded for all the world like the opening four iconic chords of Beethoven's Fifth Symphony. Da da da dum....

Could that be Joey? The call cut off right after the bangs, so maybe the boy was trying to send out a message and caught the kidnapper by surprise. Or maybe the police were right, and it was all an elaborate joke on Joey's part, with the help of an accomplice.

Drayco scanned through the notes he'd made on Mr. Jensen's business dealings. They included a list of the man's "victims," as many of the names of the desperate home-sellers Drayco could find. Then he cross-checked that list with the staff of Keirnes Boarding School he'd gotten earlier from Jennifer. One name matched both lists. It was an English teacher, the same one who owned the property next to the school.

Drayco dialed Jennifer's phone number. "I'm sorry to bother you in the middle of a meeting, but do you know if Bill Maddeaux, the English teacher, owns a piano?"

The note of annoyance in her voice quickly turned to curiosity. "I'm not sure. I've never been over to his house."

"Can I speak with him?"

"That'll be hard, I'm afraid. It's a bit of a scandal. He traveled to Colombia and was caught with a small amount of drugs at the airport on his way back. Our Headmaster thinks he'll be exonerated, but meanwhile he's stuck in a Colombian jail."

"When did he leave the U.S.?"

"Around two weeks ago."

"Is his wife home?"

"He's divorced. And lives by himself. What's going on?"

He evaded her question. "Thanks, Jennifer. You've been a big help."

Drayco closed up the laptop, scurried out of his car, and made his way toward the English teacher's property on foot. He walked along the boundary fence until it ended at another road. Could he get to the house from here? One way to find out.

He followed the road about a tenth of a mile until it branched off. One fork continued down the road, the other disappeared in the direction of the house, hidden from view by trees covered in kudzu vines. Drayco picked his way down that road until he hit the grass yard at the end of the driveway. The yard looked like a mini-jungle, not mowed in weeks.

The house itself was dark and silent. He peeked in one of the front windows. Standard living room, standard furniture. He headed toward the back and pressed his face against the glass of another room. The gold curtain covering the window had a slight gap in the middle, enough that he could see a typical study, including floor-to-ceiling shelves filled with books. It also housed one other item—a gleaming baby grand piano.

According to the school records, the English teacher, Bill Maddeaux, started working at the school three years ago. About the same time Jennifer thought the "box room" was put into use. The same box room that seemed to be punishment for only Joey.

But would one of Jensen's desperate home-sellers harbor such hatred toward the businessman they'd kidnap his son? Drayco recalled one newspaper account, where a seller likened Jensen to the devil since he singled out vulnerable homeowners without insurance. There were more articles, showing jobs lost, lives destroyed, families ripped apart. Families—maybe that was the key.

Maddeaux had a son, according to Drayco's research. William Maddeaux II. Perhaps the homeowner's son was taking revenge on the man who'd hurt his father? An eye for an eye.

Drayco pondered a little breaking and entering, but decided to check the exterior first. It was a big yard, about two acres, filled with more kudzu. It also contained the remnants of an old vineyard, fallen to the same opportunistic, choking weeds. Just like Mr. Jensen and his business practices.

In the far corner of the yard, Drayco saw a smaller vine-covered building that looked unused. If there were once any windows, they were now covered over by the vegetation. Was there a door?

Not only was there a door, some of the vines on the front appeared to be recently yanked away. He bent in closer, looking for the handle, when a voice from behind startled him. He whipped around to see Jennifer with an axe uplifted in her hand. A very large, very sharp axe.

"Jennifer, I—"

She pushed past him. "You think he's in there, don't you? I found this leaning against the house. Should make short work of those vines."

As she started whacking away, he put a hand on her arm. "It's been opened recently. Let's find the door handle."

She used the axe blade to pull more vines away from the door, enough that they could see the heavy padlock and chains keeping it shut. Wordlessly, Drayco grabbed the axe and hacked at the lock. One thwack, two thwacks, three, four...and the lock fell off.

Jennifer reached over to open the door, but again, Drayco stopped her. "Let me go in first. Just in case." Finding a body wasn't something he'd wish on anyone. He'd gotten used to it, as much as one could, but a child...those were the hardest.

He opened the door and stepped inside, as his eyes adjusted to the lack of light. The first thing he noticed was the lack of windows, just a few slivers through cracks in one corner of the ceiling. The other thing that hit him right away was the stench—an earthy rotten egg smell.

The space was larger than the box room, but not by much. The wooden bench with the hole in the back was enough to tell that this building once served as an outhouse. Next to the bench sat a rusted bowl under an equally rusted faucet with a pump, likely leading to a well. He walked over to the bench to peer into the opening. Pulling out his pocket flashlight, he shined it into the hole—signs of recent use, including several apple cores and candy wrappers.

He turned his attention to the rest of the small space. No furniture at all. Against one wall lay a blanket of leaves, but otherwise, no signs of Joey. Could he be buried inside the hole? The thought made Drayco's heart sink.

Then the blanket of leaves started to move. The head of a small boy appeared as he scooted back into a corner, away from Drayco, and clasped his arms around his knees. His wide blue eyes looked like desert oases set against his dirty, tear-smudged face. He opened his mouth, but all that came out was a squeak.

Drayco didn't move toward him, but knelt down and opened his arms to show he wasn't a threat. He looked into those blue eyes and said slowly, "Beethoven." Then he hummed, "Da da da dum."

Joey paused only a moment and then threw himself at Drayco, wrapping his arms around his neck in a bear hug. "Da da da dum," he whispered into Drayco's ear.

Jennifer joined them and smiled at Drayco as she wiped her eyes. A gust of wind through the open door made the leaves swirl around, like a dance of joy. For a moment, Drayco allowed himself to think it was the spirit of Beethoven himself, and he hugged Joey tighter.

Hugs now, food and medical attention soon. Joey had beaten the odds. Maybe that was why Drayco had a feeling this was one little music-loving boy who was going to be okay.

A Day Like No Other
Walter A.P. Soethoudt
(Translation, Willem Verhulst)

The gray skies promised yet more rain, plunging Antwerp into a mood of gloom. The British would call them "Constable skies," after the painting *Old Sarum* by John Constable, which he had seen at the Victoria and Albert Museum in London.

After seeing the painting, he had gone looking for Old Sarum and discovered it was a three-thousand-year-old settlement with a fort in the vicinity of Salisbury.

Lieutenant Belloc walked past the Pollo Loco restaurant, run by a couple of whom it was said that she was the *pollo* and he the *loco*, but that they served the best garlic chicken in the city. At the Koningin Astridplein, Belloc checked the time on his radio-controlled wristwatch against that of the Centraal Station clock. He laughed to himself, because he checked it each time he passed this way, and each time he resolved to stop doing it. When he saw a scruffy old man with a dog sitting against the front of Billiard Palace, his cap in front of him containing a few copper coins, he could not help thinking of the bad time of year that lay ahead. And that there was bound to be another load of bullshit about the homeless. He laughed wryly. Homeless, indeed. If you wanted to offer them shelter, most of them did not even want to come. Either he or she had a dog, which was not allowed into the relief center, or another smoked, which was forbidden inside the relief center, yet another drank, while the relief center's rules strictly prohibited drinking, or… He walked into fast-food restaurant Quick to see if he could get served quickly, which was the case, and within a few minutes he got his Giant and a coke.

He sat down at a small table, opened his mouth wide and took a good mouthful of his burger. He had never understood why it was called a Giant, for its size did not differ from other burgers.

He looked at a young couple with a baby and noticed the husband's attentiveness toward his wife. He used to be like that, too—attentive, tender even. He did not have to chase after her long. She had certainly been no Merlene Ottey. He started to philosophize about how it used to be between him and his wife. How crazy they were about their son and about each other. Davide had been born nine months to the day after their wedding, which elicited questions and furtive finger-counting—albeit behind their backs—by his very religious in-laws. His wife had been religious, too, and he wondered whether this had caused her reserve in sexual matters. Sometimes Belloc remarked mockingly that he would have been better off had he entered a monastery, because there would have been a greater chance of sex in there than at home.

When Davide appeared to harbor different thoughts about his own sexuality, things had started to go wrong. His wife had not accepted it and it did not take long for her to start reproaching him that their son was gay. It did not occur among the members of her family—although she would hide her disapproval from Davide. Eventually, all this led to her starting to refuse Belloc, saying that he should seek his pleasure with other women. Silently, he started calling her "Sister Clara."

He would never even have considered this, but he had been quite charmed when, at a convention of policemen and policewomen, he took the fancy of a Canadian commissioner. She reminded him of Deirdre Lovejoy, his favorite star from *The Wire*. When she made it clear—between the soup from boxes, the rubbery chicken and the grayish green beans—that he stood a chance with her, it did not take long for them to end up in bed.

She was so happy that they hit it off sexually, that she secretly put her vibrator into his suitcase. Which proved to be the start of the misery, for when he arrived home his wife was unexpectedly waiting for him, suggesting they go out to a restaurant together. Belloc could not believe his ears and suspected that she wanted to end their marriage in a gentle way, to which in principle he had no objections. But when he put down his suitcase, it started to buzz and would not stop. He wondered what it could be and opened it to find the buzzing thing. His wife also looked, and he failed to keep the buzzing vibrator hidden from her. It ended in a quarrel he did not want to see repeated. And it turned into a nasty divorce, with fights and all. It took him almost a year to win Davide back, for the boy had resolutely taken his mother's side.

Belloc took big bites of his burger and realized that he had not eaten that morning. For a moment, he looked with annoyance at a punk girl who came in, clinking on all sides. She had turned up the sound on her portable CD player to such an extent that she would probably be deaf in no time. A little while later, he walked in the direction of the Carnotstraat. Just in front of him he spotted a girl who was as thin as a leaf. She was carrying an overfull backpack, a rolled sleeping bag in her right hand and a black leather bag in her left. When he saw a man rushing toward her, Belloc closed in behind her. The man spoke English and all he asked for was "change." How stupid can you get? He quickly abandoned the attempt to help when the girl did not even look at the man and walked on unperturbedly.

Mumbling, the man then turned to Belloc, who recognized him as a one-time busker, who apparently had gone on in the world and had now reached the level of homeless beggardom.

He walked past a pub called Stad Aalst. This public house could serve as the perfect scenery for a movie based on a Charles Bukowski novel. At the corner where the Dambruggestraat and the Offerandestraat met, he turned toward the Lange Beeldekensstraat. In the Offerandestraat, a loft of pigeons were picking in vomit. Pigeons had always annoyed Belloc—he called them flying rats— and now he routed them again. This caused a passer-by to point out to Belloc that pigeons were also God's creatures.

"As far as I'm concerned they may all become Catholics," he growled. "Then maybe they will go and shit on the church."

According to Belloc, nothing remained of the former glory of the Offerandestraat. Where it used to be the street to shop for better-quality shoes, it now had become a Pakistan-cum-Indian and Moroccan junk store, with here and there a Moroccan barber, a few quick-and-dirties and an Italian restaurant run by a Bhutanese. In places, texts only in Arabic had been chalked on shop windows, and Belloc wondered what uniformed police were doing to enforce language laws in the area. Belloc resolved to have this matter raised in the city council by an alderman friend.

Some shops were even offering Ramadan discounts. The only thing that reminded Belloc of the past was the Italian clothes store Uomo, which was still selling the same quality. He did not understand how they managed to survive, for it was common knowledge that Moroccans bought at Moroccan shops and Turks at Turkish shops and nowhere else—"own people first" being their slogan, carried on into the third generation. Uomo was lucky in the sense that black people preferred Italian clothing. Belloc stopped and watched for a moment. He saw a black man enter the store, neatly dressed in a costume and wearing gold-rimmed glasses. Once, a racist friend of his had said that when a black person donned a pair of glasses, he started to behave like a left-wing intellectual. Whatever that meant, for Belloc knew few people who belonged to that category.

The farther he walked, the more he wondered if there still were any natives living here, for the white people he met usually spoke Polish or Russian, and he knew that the various emaciated drug addicts and alcoholics did not live in the district, but only came here to get their stuff. One member of the latter category was standing in front of Zeeman's, rolling a cigarette, his hands trembling as if he were suffering from Parkinson's disease. Beside him stood a dark-skinned, hook-nosed man, shouting into his cellphone like he wanted to make himself heard in North Africa or Pakistan, although it could well have been Algeria or India. Or maybe it was just to make himself heard above the din made by a group of rattling women who were greeting each other a bit farther on, sounding as if they had just covered hundreds of miles of the most impenetrable jungle to see each other.

Some vacant shops across the street looked neglected. Belloc laughed out loud when he saw a stained sign above one of the shops that said "Fresh fish daily," while on the door there was a torn piece of condensation-soaked paper that read "Closed for stock-taking." Beside it was a small shop that bought and sold all conceivable kinds of things; in its window there were a few videos with sun-bleached covers. He did not know whether it was coincidence or on purpose, but videos of *Lethal Weapon* and Hitler were lying side by side.

He walked past the house where Vincent van Gogh once lived, before he was expelled from the Antwerp academy with a report saying that he could not draw.

At home, he had a reproduction of the canvas *Skull of Skeleton with a Burning Cigarette*, which Vincent had painted during his time in Antwerp. During that period he had painted a number of canvases in the north of the city. Belloc knew—from research, as he was a great admirer of van Gogh—that Vincent had himself treated for syphilis at the Stuivenberg Hospital, which had still been under construction at the time.

A bit farther down the street, he saw a net for loose chippings against the second floor of a town house. The front of the house certainly looked damaged.

Belloc remembered his smile when he had seen a similar net on an old people's home and secretly wondered whether it was meant to catch the old ones jumping from the windows.

Because he had been looking upwards all the time, he bumped into a lad whose parents had probably come from somewhere in an African country.

Angry with himself, Belloc said, "Please accept my apologies."

"You did that on purpose," said the boy defiantly.

"Now listen to me, son," Belloc said, suddenly both father and cop, "just fuck off and go home. Your mother has fried fish ready." While saying this, he could not help laughing at himself, wondering how long ago it was since he had last used that expression, which used to be a common saying in Antwerp at one time.

"I'll report you to the police for racism," the lad said.

"Do as you please. You are the ones to talk of racism! Arabs look down on Berbers, Turks on Kurds, Moroccans call Algerians and Tunisians thieves, Senegalese say that Congolese are monkeys and Ugandans hate Ghanese and vice versa, while the whole of Africa is collectively against Nigeria, and you think you're the ones who should make comments," Belloc growled, stepping aside and, ignoring the boy, walked on.

Across the street, Belloc saw a small panel truck parked near a grocery shop, advertising Casablanca-Moroccan Lager 5%. At the same time, he saw a man dressed in a djellaba with the hood turned up put something on the side of the truck and, a little later, also on the grocer's shop window.

The man disappeared as quickly as he had come.

Belloc crossed the street and read:

KORAN 5
Al-Ma'idah

Verse 91: Certainly Satan desires to cast enmity and hatred among you by wine and gambling, and to hinder you from the remembrance of Allah, and from prayer.

Suddenly, Belloc felt a sharp pain. He tried to turn, but he was grabbed, while somebody pushed the knife further into his back and somebody else whispered in his ear, "Racist."

Our Gallery of Suspects

Herschel Cozine

Herschel Cozine has published extensively in both children and adult publications. Work by Herschel has also appeared in *Alfred Hitchcock* and *Ellery Queen's Mystery Magazines, Sherlock Holmes Magazine*, Wolfmont Press Toys for Tots Anthologies and *Woman's World*. His story, "A Private Hanging" was a finalist for the Derringer award. Herschel has published numerous short stories with Untreed Reads, and his Nurseyland Crimes stories have been combined into a collection, along with new stories, titled *The Osgood Case Files*. He also appears in *The Killer Wore Cranberry: A Second Helping* and *The Killer Wore Cranberry: Room for Thirds.*

Bobbi A. Chukran

Bobbi A. Chukran is a native Texan author of mystery and suspense fiction and an award-winning playwright. She's the author of *Lone Star Death*, the "Nameless, Texas" series, *Halloween Thirteen, Dye Dyeing Dead* and others. Her work has been published in 'zines such as *Mysterical-E, Dark Eclipse, Kings River Life, Over My Dead Body, Mystery Reader's Journal* and in several anthologies. Bobbi blogs about her stories and inspiration at http://bobbichukran.blogspot.com.

Su Kopil

Su Kopil's short stories have appeared in numerous publications including: *Destination Mystery* (DarkhouseBooks), *Fish or Cut Bait* (WildsidePress), *Woman's World Magazine*, and *Over My Dead Body*. A book cover designer, dog devotee, and bibliophile, you can find her online at sukopil.com or follow her on twitter @INKspillers.

P.A. De Voe

P.A. De Voe is a cultural anthropologist, which accounts for her being an incorrigible magpie for collecting seemingly irrelevant information. She writes contemporary and historical mysteries—the latter take place in 14th and 15th century China. The *Judge Lu Ming Dynasty Case Files* is a set of short stories modeled after crime stories traditionally written by Chinese magistrates themselves. P.A. De Voe's teen ancient China adventure/mystery trilogy features a magistrate's bi-racial daughter whose world is turned upside down when an enemy accuses her father of treason.

Laurie Stevens

Laurie Stevens is a novelist, screenwriter and playwright. Her debut novel *The Dark Before Dawn,* is the first in the Gabriel McRay psychological suspense series. *Deep into Dusk* is the second. The two books have earned nine awards including the Kirkus Star, being named to Kirkus Reviews Best of 2011, and the 2014 Silver IPPY award for Best Mystery/Thriller. Laurie is a hybrid author, first independently publishing her books, then securing an agent and obtaining a two-book deal with Random House, Germany. *Todes Schuld* makes its debut in 2015. An active member of Mystery Writers of America and International Thriller Writers, Laurie also sits on the Board of Sisters in Crime, Los Angeles. Her short stories have appeared in numerous magazines and e-zines including the anthology, *Last Exit to Murder.* To learn more about the author, visit her website at http://www.lauriestevensbooks.com.

Tim Wohlforth

Tim is the author of three Jim Wolf novels. Wolf lives on a boat at Jack London Square in Oakland with Monty, an eight-foot-long Burmese python. The latest novel, *The Curse of the Chameleon,* has just been published by Krill. It begins with the murder of an American Indian and ends in Macau. Another book, *The Pink Tarantula,* features Crip and Henrietta. Tom Bateman, a paraplegic PI, can't get rid of his green-haired, pierced "helper." *Harry,* a standalone, deals with eco-terrorism. Over 80 of his short stories have been published. Four of his books are available in audio format. www.timwohlforth.com.

Suzanne Berube Rorhus

Suzanne Berube Rorhus writes from the arctic clime known as Michigan, though she still guards her Southern accent carefully. Her work includes "The Golden Ganesh," which appeared in *Ellery*

Queen Mystery Magazine; Cereal Killer (available from Untreed Reads); "A Murder Far from Home," as part of the Untreed Reads anthology *Moon Shot: Murder and Mayhem on the Edge of Space*, and *Cuffed*, a series of true tales written with a police officer coauthor. She is now working on a police procedural novel.

Sandra Murphy

Sandra lives in the land of shoes, booze and blues, St. Louis, Missouri. On a hot summer day, the smell of hops from the brewery stirs up the voices in her head, clamoring to get out. She lives with her faithful companion, Ozzie, a Westie-ish dog, who doesn't mind listening while she talks to her characters. She has had several short stories published as standalones through Untreed Reads, including "Bananas Foster," "Sweet Tea and Deviled Eggs," "The Obituary Rule" and "Superstition."

Julie Tollefson

Julie Tollefson grew up in the sand hills of Southwest Kansas, where she landed her first paying writing gig investigating such hard-hitting stories as "Do blondes really have more fun?" for her hometown newspaper. She's a regular contributor to *Lawrence Magazine,* and her short fiction has appeared in *Alfred Hitchcock Mystery Magazine* and *Fish Nets: The Second Guppy Anthology*. She's a member of Sisters in Crime and Mystery Writers of America. She and her family live in northeast Kansas. Visit her online at http://julietollefson.com, or follow her on Twitter, @jtollefson.

O'Neil De Noux

O'Neil De Noux has 31 books in print, and over 300 short story sales in multiple genres: crime fiction, historical fiction, children's fiction, mainstream fiction, science-fiction, suspense, fantasy, horror, western, literary, young adult, religious, romance, humor and erotica. His fiction has received several awards, including the Shamus Award for Best Short Story, the Derringer Award for Best Novelette and the 2011 Police Book of the Year. Two of his stories have appeared in the Best American Mystery Stories anthology

(2013 and 2007). He is a past Vice-President of the Private Eye Writers of America.

John M. Floyd

John M. Floyd's work has appeared in more than 200 different publications, including *The Strand Magazine, Alfred Hitchcock's Mystery Magazine, Ellery Queen's Mystery Magazine, Woman's World* and *The Saturday Evening Post.* A former Air Force captain and IBM systems engineer, he won a Derringer Award in 2007, and was nominated for an Edgar Award in 2015. One of his stories was selected by publisher Otto Penzler and guest editor James Patterson for inclusion in *The Best American Mystery Stories 2015,* and another has been chosen for the upcoming *Mississippi Noir* (Akashic Books). John is also the author of six books: *Rainbow's End, Midnight, Clockwork, Deception, Fifty Mysteries* and *Dreamland* (coming in 2016). He is the author of the standalone short stories "The Early Death of Pinto Bishop" and "Watched," both published by Untreed Reads.

JoAnne Lucas

Bio of a blonde:

JoAnne Lucas writes of the Fresno/Clovis, California area of the great San Joaquin Valley. She has long been a member of Mystery Writers of America, Private Eye Writers of America and Sisters in Crime. Her stories can be found in print and electronic anthologies such as *Valley Fever—Where Murder Is Contagious, A Woman's Touch, Destination: Mystery, DIME* and others.

Andrew MacRae

Andrew MacRae is the author of two novels, *Murder Misdirectd,* and its sequel, *Murder Miscalculated,* both featuring a former pickpocket who cannot keep from getting into trouble. In addition to numerous short stories, he has recently curated and edited several anthologies, including, *Destination: Mystery!* from Darkhouse Books. Through Untreed Reads he has published a short story collection titled *The Case of the Murderous Mermaid and Other Stories,* and he appears in the Untreed Reads anthologies *Moon Shot: Murder and Mayhem on the Edge of Space* and *The Killer Wore Cranberry: A Second Helping*.

Judy Penz Sheluk

Judy Penz Sheluk's debut mystery novel, *The Hanged Man's Noose* (Barking Rain Press) was published in July 2015. Her short crime fiction is included in *The Whole She-Bang 2* (Toronto Sisters in Crime) and *World Enough and Crime* (Carrick Publishing).

In her less mysterious pursuits, Judy works as a freelance writer/editor. She is currently Editor of Home *BUILDER Magazine* and Senior Editor of *New England Antiques Journal*.

In addition to the Short Fiction Mystery Society, Judy is a member of Sisters in Crime (International/Toronto/Guppies), Crime Writers of Canada, and International Thriller Writers. Find her at www.judypenzsheluk.com, where she interviews other writers and blogs about the writing life.

Albert Tucher

Albert Tucher is the creator of prostitute Diana Andrews, who has appeared in more than sixty short stories in such venues as *ThugLit*, *Shotgun Honey* and *The Best American Mystery Stories 2010*, edited by Lee Child. Diana's first longer case, the novella *The Same Mistake Twice*, was published by Untreed Reads in 2013. Albert's work also appears in the Untreed Reads anthologies *The Untreed Detectives* and *Discount Noir*, as well as the standalone short stories *Calories*, *The Retro Look* and *Value for the Money*, all of which feature Diana. Albert Tucher works at the Newark Public Library, where he is legendary for his coffee consumption.

Earl Staggs

Earl Staggs earned a long list of Five Star reviews for his novels *Memory of a Murder* and *Justified Action*, and has twice received a Derringer Award for Best Short Story of the Year. He served as Managing Editor of *Futures Mystery Magazine*, as President of the Short Mystery Fiction Society, and is a frequent speaker at conferences and seminars. Several of Earl's short stories appear in the Untreed Reads anthologies *The Killer Wore Cranberry, The Killer*

Wore Cranberry: A Second Helping and *The Killer Wore Cranberry: A Fourth Meal of Mayhem,* as well as several standalone shorts. He welcomes any comments via email at earlstaggs@sbcglobal.net and invites you to visit his blog site at http://earlwstaggs.wordpress.com.

Barb Goffman

Barb Goffman's *Don't Get Mad, Get Even* (Wildside Press 2013) won the Silver Falchion Award for best short-story collection of 2013. Barb also won the 2013 Macavity Award for best short story, and she's been nominated fifteen times for national crime-writing awards, including the Agatha, Anthony, and Macavity awards. When not writing, Barb runs a freelance editing and proofreading service, focusing on crime and general fiction. Barb's short stories appear in all four volumes of the Untreed Reads *The Killer Wore Cranberry* anthology series. Learn more at www.barbgoffman.com.

BV Lawson

Author, poet and journalist BV Lawson's award-winning work has appeared in dozens of publications and anthologies. A four-time Derringer Award finalist and 2012 winner for her short fiction, BV was also honored by the American Independent Writers and Maryland Writers Association for her Scott Drayco series, with the debut novel, *Played To Death,* named Best Mystery in the 2015 Next Generation Indie Book Awards and a Shamus Award finalist. Scott Drayco also features in the Untreed Reads standalone short story *Ill-Gotten* Games. BV currently lives in Virginia with her husband and enjoys flying above the Chesapeake Bay in a little Cessna. Visit her website and sign up for her newsletter at bvlawson.com. No ticket required.

Walter Soethoudt

Born in Antwerp, Flanders, September 20, 1939, and married for 48 years to Nadine Megan Lusyne, Walter was a publisher for 47 years. He turned to a career as Literary Agent who handles full-length fiction and nonfiction, with a special interest in crime, suspense, thrillers and films noir.

His publications include *Uitgevers komen in de hemel* (2008); *Publishers Go to Heaven*, his memoires; *De nacht die de dag vergat* (2012)—Dutch; *The Night Who Forgot the Day*, a story about the first 4 months of 1916 in WW I, starting in the trenches of Flanders and ending in the Easter Rising in Dublin. He is also working on the not-yet-published 4th part of a series called *Dark Past* (about films noir and everything that goes with it—blacklisting, redlisting, etc.).

Walter is an Honorary Member of the Vereniging van de Vlaamse Filmpers (Flemish Film Press), and Honorary Member of Boek.be (the Flemish trade organization for editors, booksellers and importers).